SHARING THE TROUGH

PETER LLOYD-DAVIES

iUNIVERSE, INC.
NEW YORK   BLOOMINGTON

Sharing the Trough

iUniverse books may be ordered through booksellers or by contacting:

iUniverse
1663 Liberty Drive
Bloomington, IN 47403
www.iuniverse.com
1-800-Authors (1-800-288-4677)

ISBN: 978-1-4401-8448-2 (sc)
ISBN: 978-1-4401-8452-9 (ebk)

Printed in the United States of America

iUniverse rev. date: 12/09/2009

I

"Get a move on you two. This place is like a pig sty. You've got fifteen minutes to finish here before going down to the mess for breakfast."

This was just like every other morning. The two occupants of the prison cell hurriedly finished tidying up before making their way along the gallery of the first floor of block 'A'. The officer bellowed the order to the two unfortunate occupants of cell sixteen. The only thing worse than the routine demands of the prison officers was the constant bullying by the 'hard men' of the place. These were the *Lifers,* the murderers and rapists destined to spend a large slice of their lives serving out the 'life' sentences the courts had sentenced them to for the awful crimes they had been convicted of..

"McCormick, you and O'Reilly report to me as soon as you finish eating and don't take all damn day about it."

The two of them were used to this kind of language from their keepers. . "Yes sir, Officer Corbett."

McCormick responded to the brusque command. O'Reilly nodded his acknowledgement of the order.

The two of them spent most of their working days together on the prison farm. Sean O'Reilly was the only inmate with any previous experience of farming, and so a natural choice by the governor to look after the unit.

Martin O'Reilly, Sean's father, had built up a pig breeding and fattening plant and it was on this place that Sean had spent the whole of his childhood helping with the chores.

O'Reilly and McCormick had the daily job to feed all the animals and to establish a state of cleanliness regarding the pig unit, which was almost superior to the conditions of most of the prison inmates quarters! At this task the two of them excelled.

Sean's father died two years before Sean O'Reilly was imprisoned. This had had a devastating effect on a young man who had lost his mother during his birth and now, having lost his father he was the only one to look after the animals. He was capable of doing this, but it was a lonely existence. His 'cousin' Rachel Flanagan, who was a frequent visitor to the farm, volunteered to be his regular assistant and she moved into the spare room at the cottage to be constantly available for the essential tasks. This made the situation much easier. She was a pretty sixteen year old with old fashioned values and little interest in the things most of her school friends indulged in.

Rachel's mother had her own business in the Republic which was on the shadier side of grey in terms of legality! Nellie was the producer of illegal liquid sustenance known locally as 'potcheen' or poteen. A harsh version of Irish Whiskey. At this, she was the proud local expert. Her daughter didn't approve of the liquor or its manufacture and was pleased to have the opportunity to escape to 'Uncle' Martin,s pig farm. Besides….. she had a big crush on Sean!

2

The twenty third of February 1961. Sean O'Reilly had reached the last day of his sentence at the prison on Crumlin Road in Belfast. He was twenty one years old and was eager to get on with the rest of his life.

Five feet ten inches tall with dark, wavy hair. his eyes a deep azure blue, made him very popular with all the girls he met. He was considered by these lassies to be a fit looking fella!

It took only a few minutes to end his fragile associations with his fellow inmates before his release. There was little he had in common with most of them. However, there was one individual he enjoyed a joke with, who seemed to be more of a kindred spirit and whom he had spent his incarceration working with, who hailed from the same area of this tortured province of Northern Ireland.

This character enjoyed the overused handle - 'Paddy' preceding his surname; McCormick. Patrick Morgan McCormick's address and home telephone number were written on the inside of an empty cigarette packet Sean found in the palm of his hand after their farewell handshake.

The gate warder closed the solid oak doors behind him. He heard the familiar noise of keys clinking on their chain before the sound of the lock being engaged ended his incarceration.

Sean had just spent the last two years of his young life in that prison. He had been caught whilst shifting forty gallons of the finest Potcheen from 'Aunt' Nellie's illicit distillery at Kilmona, in the peaceful countryside of County Cork, to its usual destination Enniskillen, for onward distribution. After years of dodging the Garda south of the border and Ulster Constabulary's finest in the north, he was finally caught with a forty gallon drum hidden in the bulk of the muck spreader which he was towing behind his clapped-out Land-Rover. Having used this mode of transport with success for several years, Sean was surprised and a little annoyed when he was stopped by a constable near Enniskillen, who insisted on having the load emptied in a nearby field.

"Well now Officer," he said. "Who do I send the bill to?"

" What bill?"

"For the valuable shit!"

The line was not lost on the officer who admired the quick thinking of the scruffy individual leaning on the gate of the meadow now gorging a ton and a half of sweet smelling pig dung.

The clatter of the heavy oil drum being tumbled end over end as the feed chain propelled it towards the spreader flails at the rear of the manure spreader as it was being emptied told the story, and sealed his fate.

3

A last quick glance at the closed gate of the prison, Sean turned away and strolled across the road to the bus stop to begin a journey back to his roots and the pig farm. The farm was on an ex wartime RAF airfield. Most of the concrete buildings had been converted into pens suitable for producing and rearing pigs. One of these buildings near the entrance to the aerodrome had been converted into a small cottage-style home for the use of the tenant. Some of the other buildings were empty and had remained neglected since the base closed some years earlier.

After a two and a half hour ride from Belfast, Sean stepped down from the warmth of the bus into the winter afternoon. He found himself shivering from the bitterly cold wind slashing like frozen whips across his shoulders and ripping through his uncovered hair. There was a three mile struggle with this unwelcome companion before he would arrive at the farm, where there was no guarantee that he would be welcome. Two years was a long absence from seven hundred pigs, always looking hopefully for food and a young girl who was only there to 'help with the chores' !

Sean's 'cousin' Rachel, had reluctantly agreed to look after the place for a day or two when he was sent down. By now, Sean surmised, Rachel would have fallen for these lovely creatures, or she would kill *him*. Probably both!

Although they had been writing regularly, he had no idea how she had been able to manage to keep the farm going on her own and he was feeling guilty about the whole business. Her letters were always up-beat. Probably intended to help him keep his spirits up during his 'holiday'.

After the uncomfortable walk from the bus, his breath produced clouds of vapour as he stood on the step of the cottage. How will she react to his arrival? Whilst he stood there wondering what this was going to be, he didn't notice the curtain being pushed aside in the window behind him. Suddenly the door was open….. Standing in the frame of the door lit by the single electric light above her head, was the beautiful colleen he last saw when she was only sixteen. Her shoulder length auburn hair shone where the light from the weak bulb caught it. She was still only five feet six inches tall but she had lost the puppy fat cheeks he remembered. Now her high cheekbones gave her slim face a staggering beauty which surprised and excited him.

"So. It's you is it Sean," she said as she dragged him into the tiny space pretending to be the hallway of the cottage.

"'Tis a long couple of days so it is!"

Then she kissed him full on the mouth. After Sean had recovered from his surprise she went on; "Will you be staying a little time then. You know, to help with the animals?"

She looked at him with a raised eyebrow and a cheeky smile spread across her lovely face. It wasn't often that he found difficulty in finding the right words.

He could usually express himself eloquently. Not now though. As he stood open-mouthed staring at this young beauty he was surprised at his inability to find the words to express his gratitude for all she been doing for him, and for this totally unexpected welcome.

"Rachel , I really want to try and put things right", was all he was able to respond.

"I'm sure you will", she said, looking at him with her wide hazel eyes from under her long, dark eyelashes.

"Holy Mother of God" he whispered, more to himself rather than to her.

"So am I going to get a straight answer then? " she enquired.

"About what?" he said.

"About whether you intend staying on here, or moving on to some other daft idea of yours. You *are* going to stop playing with Mum's giggle-juice aren't you?" He was silent for a time, thinking.

"What do you want me to do?" he asked.

"All the time you were away I was thinking about you, hoping that you would come back and want me to be with you to help run this place" Rachel responded. Sean couldn't believe his ears. When he last spoke to her she seemed somewhat remote. The warmth of her words came as a surprise. He made up his mind that he would never again put himself in a compromising position, the farm would be his only job. Well, after she warned him that she would never speak to him again if he wouldn't give up the 'other nonsense'. The promise she was offering couldn't be ignored. Time, it's said, cures. It now looked as though the girl had forgotten the bitter fight they had had before he set out that last time. Sean hadn't forgotten though, he could still feel the pain from the hot stew burning his face as it came from the pan-full straight from the stove and which she had so accurately aimed at his head! The mental pain from having upset her so much was etched deep into his mind. During those long, lonely nights in prison, he wished he had listened to her, he was not overly upset by having been caught, or even being sent to that violent place, it was the senseless waste of time and the loss of her company which hurt so much. It was decision time. Of course he wanted to stay at the farm. It was now unthinkable to move on, to search for something he knew didn't exist. A better life….. What could be better than this? Sean moved close to this wonderful person and put his arms around her waist , drew her to him and gently brushed his trembling lips against hers. She responded to his tender advance with a passion that Sean had never known in his life. Her hands caressed his flushed cheeks as she held his handsome face between them. The evening of tenderness which followed, made them both realise how much they had missed each other.

4

The farm was now in the process of expansion. Six three titted cows, those which had suffered from mastitis in one of the 'quarters' of its udder, had been purchased from a 'rough' dealer south of the border. This tinker was known to both of their families as 'one to use but not to befriend', as aunty Nellie regularly stated but he was useful to people like the young couple as there were few places where it was possible to purchase cheaply, animals which with care, could produce an income for the farm. Although it was well managed it had constant cash-flow problems.

Monthly visits, cap-in-hand to the bank manager Mr Jones, were necessary when support with overdraft or loans were required. Mr Jones was a junior trainee assistant manager. His purpose in the bank was to be responsible for interviewing the 'risky' clients. Mostly those from the farming fraternity who were trying to obtain loans for their poorly managed smallholdings.

It was always a very uncomfortable half hour. Sean, highly scrubbed, suited and booted, seated across the mahogany desk from the pompous bespectacled jumped-up clerk who dictated his poverty. This was the sort of individual Sean detested. The only conversation which ever passed between them was a 'servant and master' confrontation, almost always ending with a lecture in 'prudence', with the master admonishing the 'little man' for allowing the overdraft to exceed the previous order by five quid! 'Allowing this to happen every other month is the road to financial disaster', was a frequently repeated quote which had become a cliché. Sean always left these sessions feeling depressed and inadequate. Rachel usually had the antidote ready for him! This unfortunate relationship with the bank and its officials had a deep effect on Sean, and he could often be found cursing one or other of these people when a foot was trodden on by a cow, or a sow was behaving awkwardly, as they often did. It was always the bank's fault! There was no point in blaming the misbehaving animal, or machine or whatever, far better to get any annoyance off the chest with a short burst of anti-bank vernacular.

The routine duties on the farm were shared between the two of them. As they were both very fond of all animals, particularly pigs. .

5

Rachel and Sean were soon a popular couple in their neighbourhood, they took part in all the social events, enjoyed the dances at the village hall and went to Mass most Sundays. As a result, many friends were made and some of these would visit the farm during the summer evenings. It was always a treat to show off the sows and gilts with their babies, particularly the very new born. It was fun to take the children of friends to the farrowing houses (where the sows produced their off-spring). These were friendly places with a gentle aroma, un- like the fattening houses where hundreds of young animals were kept to be fattened for bacon or pork. Opening the door to the house as quietly as possible, creeping in trying not to disturb the peace of dozens of slumbering animals. It was wonderful to hear the sounds of squeaks, grunts and squeals from pigs 'doing their thing'.

'Aren't they gorgeous', would be the usual comment from the visitors at first sight of a line of living sausages piled on top of each other fast asleep, eyes shut with eyelashes a supermodel would die for! During the first few weeks of their lives the tiny piglets were drawn by the light and warmth of infra-red floodlights suspended above the steel bars which formed the 'creep', the safety zone which allowed the vulnerable young animals to escape from possible crushing by their otherwise protective parent. Rachel and Sean loved it when it was quiet like this at night, the sound of ten or eleven piglets attacking the milk-bar with a chorus of sucking and grunting, squealing and squabbling as each baby scrambled over its siblings to change position in order to find the most productive tap! Many squabbles developed as a result of these actions.

There was always work to do which at times proved very tiring to them both. Rachel had to look after the household chores and would always assist Sean when these were done. Their courting would have suffered if they were employed at the same hectic level in any other job. The answer to any lack of enthusiasm by either partner was to insist on a visit to the boar house for inspiration !

6

One February evening they were sitting in front of the fire in their cosy parlour. The light was off and they were unusually quiet. Firelight danced around the room, an occasional spark would fly out of the fire thrown by an angry log which seemed to be objecting to being disposed of like this just to keep these humans sitting opposite warm.

"I think we'll have to see what else we can do to improve the cash-flow if we want to enjoy a more exciting lifestyle" said Sean

"Maybe I could get an evening job".

"Doing what ; exactly?" Rachel replied.

"I was hoping you could come up with that" he said. Rachel was quick to tell him that she already possessed everything she wanted. He was pleased that he hadn't said anything about his earlier thoughts it would have ruined the moment. A proposal of marriage would have to wait though, whatever he said to her now he would have to be careful. Asking her to marry him would probably spoil the relationship which was developing between them. Sean knew she would always have regrets if they didn't do it 'properly' especially as her Catholic background almost demanded the union should be recognised with a traditional white dress.

Sean's priority now was to improve the performance of their business to secure their future. A Catholic marriage would expect production of children, these were expensive! After making this decision, all that was required was a pragmatic plan to develop ways of finding a sustainable increase in funds.

There was a growing market at this time among the more affluent in British society for the meat of rare breeds of domestic animals. Highland cattle, Manx Loughtan sheep and Gloucester Old Spot pigs amongst them. The contacts he had established already in livestock circles, were explored once again.

Following a series of telephone calls to selected breeders, a trip to the local bank to challenge the upstart trainee manager to part with a substantial loan was arranged. As usual his request was studied for a full minute before being rejected, Sean decided not to allow this idiot of a bank clerk to lecture him once again about a subject of which he was ignorant. Another waste of time. After repeated attempts to influence the jobs-worth at the bank, in spite of a well planned business idea Sean realised that if funds were going to be found to proceed with his programme he would have to look elsewhere. Returning to the farm frustration had unsettled him.

He decided not to tell Rachel that he had been refused funds yet again, there was only one solution to this stalemate. Well aware of the reaction he would get if Rachel ever found out. He knew the only way out of the impasse was to find an alternative method of fundraising. A phone call to aunty Nellie was the next move.

"Hello Nellie, how are things in the deep south?"

She was a little surprised to hear his voice after what had been ages since they had last spoken. Nellie had been trying to persuade her 'nephew' to return to the removal business ever since he had been released from his enforced 'holiday'!

"Will you be giving me another dose of ear-ache or do you want something?" she said.

"No, no, nothing like that. I thought you might like to know how your daughter is, that's all. She misses your nonsense even if she despises what you do!"

"I cannot understand that girl, she had a fine education as a result of the profit made by the business".

If Rachel's father had survived the 'troubles' and not got himself killed, everything would have been very different. The mix-up with Danny Kelly over the price of a few gallons of Nellie's best and the stupid fight which caused Joe to have his heart attack seemed such a waste of a valuable life.

"Can I not persuade you to shift a few more pints then?"

"That's why I'm calling you so it is", said Sean.

"You mean you *will?*" Nellie said, her voice rising in the excitement of a possible resumption of business.

"No Nell, I wouldn't dare! not after my promise to Rachel. I'm sure you don't want another row with her do you? I think we can do business without me being personally involved". The disappointment in her voice was clear to Sean when she replied;

"There was me getting all excited about seeing my lovely handsome boyo again"

"You'll be doing that Nellie, I'm coming down to see you this afternoon."

Rachel was waiting for him after his visit to the bank, eager to find out how the meeting went with their unpopular bank manager.

"How went it then?" was the greeting as he went into the kitchen where Rachel was preparing lunch for them both.

"My but something smells good!" Sean replied. trying to change the subject. He was a poor liar, but now he had to convince her that at last, the idiot manager had seen sense. He knew that he wouldn't be able to continue to convince her, something would give him away but, for now, he could work out his plan.

"Yeah OK" was his vague response to her question.

Lunch was the important thing to consider right now, later he would find a way of telling her the truth but not at this particular moment.

"Are you ready yet, its on the table" she called out.

"Coming love", he replied as he was drying himself after washing his hands. Just as she was setting the steaming pot on the table he came into the room. Once again he remembered the last time he was in trouble with her.

"Well, what did Mr Jones say after he gave you the loan?" she enquired.

"Not much, only that he'd never seen a presentation like it in all his business life!"

This wasn't far from the truth. Sean didn't enjoy lying to her like this and he knew it would rebound on him, at the time it seemed the only way he could still marry the girl was to get his breeding stock soon, or the farm may fail. Failure was not on his agenda.

That afternoon on the pretext of visiting the livestock show, which was co-incidentally taking place that day over in Armagh, he took the old Austin out of the barn, kept there to make it last longer rather than for security or elegance, and drove out of the gate leaving a trail of blue smoke.

7

Sean was heading south to keep his appointment with auntie Nellie in Kilmona. The journey was long and tiring. Sean wished he could have brought Rachel with him. Effort must be made to get these two talking again family ties were so important. Sean had lost all his own.

The roads in the south were more like cart-tracks than highways fit for motorcars and the old Austin objected to the treatment its owner was subjecting it to.

There was no way that the old jalopy and Sean were going to be able to return that day, obviously Rachel would have to be telephoned after he arrived at Nellie's and a suitable reason would have to be invented for staying away over-night. Sean didn't possess the 'gift of the gab' usually associated with the average Irishman. It was going to test him to the limit to make a convincing story to present to Rachel. The obvious lie would be to tell her the Austin had broken down.... Again! It had happened many times in the past year but he would have to tell another whopper the following day when he would be away for a second night. 'Why didn't I just tell her the truth? Heck no. Is the Pope Catholic?'

Nellie's place was a traditional Irish cottage with a small parcel of land consisting of a collection of paddocks. In the past these had been the homes of assorted livestock, mainly working horses, with an occasional donkey used for transport.

Now, these little patches were neglected derelict weed gardens. The cottage itself was accessed via an overgrown track which led off a mainly disused lane which was in desperate need of attention from a caring council, which didn't exist. The place was so isolated hardly anyone in the local area knew of its existence which made it ideal for the illicit purpose to which Nellie had put it. Sean was of course was familiar with the area as he had been there many times since his youth. He was relieved to have arrived in one piece.

The 'main' roads for want of a more accurate description, were even worse than he remembered. There were pot-holes wide enough and deep enough to bury a dead cart-horse together with its cart! It sometimes seemed as though these craters were joined together. A very rough journey. Tired as he was he was anxious to discuss with Nellie the possibility of 'doing a little business' knowing that herself was also very keen.

8

Sean reached the front door just as it opened. Although he hadn't seen her for quite a while he could see that she was still just the same. She stood a full five feet two inches in her shoes, still had her grey hair in a bun and the gold rimmed spectacles that she wore were perched on the end of her nose as usual.

Her green eyes still sparkled when she smiled, which was often. Now in her fifties, she had a soft complexion typical of her generation in this part of Eire.

"So I'm thinking you're after some pennies young Sean?"

"Aye, that I am Nell"

"Well come inside and let's chew the fat."

After enjoying a large Jack Daniels, Sean brought her up to date with the goings-on at the farm, telling her that Rachel had no idea that he'd come down to Cork.

"She thinks I'm at the Armagh show" he explained that Rachel would skin him alive if she knew what he was contemplating.

"Sure, and she'll not learn from me son" Nellie replied.

"I wish the pair of you would try to mend those fences". Sean almost pleaded with Nellie. This unpleasant rift would have to be dealt with soon. It was imperative to Sean that the relationship between mother and daughter be mended.

"I have a contact up north who I think will do the runs Nell. I'm not going to risk getting caught. If we pay him half of my normal cut for each delivery I'm sure he'll be happy."

" What's he like then? is he a good Catholic?

" I'm sure you'll get on with him fine . I'll send him down to meet you before you organise the next job." They chatted late into the night and Sean was satisfied that the next few weeks would see enough liquor swilling up to the province to provide more that enough capital to acquire the boar and a couple of top quality gilts which would be required to start building up the new herd which, he was sure, would see the start of their fortune. To be clear of the stupid ignoramus Jones, would make the risk he was taking very worth while.

He was awake early. The full moon was shining through the net curtains in Nellie's spare bedroom. It was this which woke him and he was grateful for it.

An early start would see him back at the farm in time for tea.

He had only been away for a day so far, but it seemed much longer. Sean hated what he was having to do, particularly lying to Rachel as he had, but he was now determined to improve their lifestyle and be able to ask her to marry him.

The old car didn't let him down on the return journey in spite of the cruel treatment he had given it. A lunch break at Tulach Mhor gave them both a rest from the punishment.

The tired old wreck (the car, not himself,) came to a grateful rest at four fifteen, in time to take over the feeding duty. A quick change into his mucky working gear and he was ready to face the music. "Where on earth have you been , have you had an accident ?" Rachel demanded.

"The bloody car broke down didn't it." The plan was coming apart already , she knew he was telling a porky.

"Pull the other one Sean, I *know* the car didn't let you down!" He didn't expect this sort of welcome. If he had, he would have found a better answer. How the hell did she know?

had Nellie said something? If only he'd given her a phone call last night.

"What do you mean?" was all he could say.

"You were seen! " Sean couldn't believe it. He had been so careful, told no-one except Nellie that he was visiting her, and she had promised him that nothing would ever persuade her to jeopardise their clandestine plans for mutual financial benefit. 'Where could I possibly have been seen?' he asked himself, after all the only place he could have been observed was at the roadside eating house and he had only stopped for a short break.

"Please Sean don't deny it. I know where you have been and I want to know what you went to Mum's for." She demanded.

"OK yeah, I have been to Nellie's. I lied to you the other day. Our friend at the bank will not help us as usual, and if the farm is to survive we must find the necessary cash for those fresh animals The only way that I can get it is to help your mum to shift a little more stuff. Anyway who did see me and where was I seen?" He queried.

"Oh Sean how could you? You know how I feel about you risking what we have, by getting involved with mum again." Sean felt very uncomfortable.

"I know that, but you have to understand that I want us to live with a bit more dignity. If I can get those pigs for breeding we will be able to sell all the spare progeny and all the pork we can produce."

He tried to justify his deception by suggesting a promising future as a result of his actions.

"I thought I'd made it perfectly clear to you that I would rather live in a pig-sty than wait for you again! I mean it Sean, I will *not* try to run this place again on my own it's not right and it's not fair of you to expect me to."

" You're right, which is why I will not be taking the risk of doing the job myself. I plan to persuade that guy I was in prison with, the one I told you about so often, Paddy Mc Cormick, I'm sure he'll be keen to do it.

We talked a lot about it inside and he seemed really excited about the whole idea. Running rings around themselves would be a big part of the attraction for him."

"It's bad enough you lying to me, without getting someone who I've never met doing your dirty work for you." Rachel shouted, "How do we know he won't screw you , or dump you in to the R.U.C. again?" She responded.

"I've thought about all that. I'm sure he'll have a darned sight more to lose than me. The cops would have a hard job proving I'm involved if I don't go anywhere near the job."

"Don't be so stupid Sean."

"Look, I'm going to do this there's no other way, it'll only need two or three runs to get the cash we need. As soon as we have enough I'll put a stop to it I promise."

"I'm warning you now, if you don't give this idea up you can find somewhere else to live!"

It was getting cold outside now. Late autumn in the Province always brought an almost constant downpour. The temperature in the cottage was colder still, frosty would describe it better. 'Saints preserve me' he said to himself as he slammed the door shut behind him leaving his lovely Rachel crying. He was determined to carry out his plan. Tomorrow he would give Paddy a ring and be damned...... He probably would be!

With angry thoughts tumbling through his mind, he turned up his collar and strode purposefully towards the first of the buildings where his noisy friends waited in anticipation of being fed. As usual as soon as they heard the latch being moved they let him know they were ready. As one they began to bellow their approval of his arrival. When they had all stuffed their eager snouts into their troughs he let himself out of the building and repeated the process as he progressed from shed to shed satisfying each animal in his care. It took him nearly an hour to go round them all before re - tracing his steps, by which time he had calmed down and hoped Rachel would have done the same.

Sean should have known this would not be the case, he'd been here before. She was as mad as he had ever seen her. Her face was tear-stained, but he could easily see the anger behind those eyes. The anger he could cope with. The hurting though, was something else. Rachel was well aware that her man was a real softie and in her own way was quite sorry for him. She also knew that his motive was totally un-selfish. This time she had to let him know that she was too upset to soon forgive him, or her mother for getting him involved again.

"Get out! you can sleep with your precious pigs tonight. You're just like them!"

He knew there would be no reasoning with her when she was like this. He snatched his spare raincoat from its hook in the porch and accepted the harsh inevitability of his predicament as he made his way once more across the yard towards the relative warmth of the farrowing house and its friendly occupants.

He spent quite a while enjoying the sights and sounds of these familiar creatures before making a rough job of his temporary bed amongst the straw bales. He was surprised how comfortable it was and he was pleased that he didn't have to go back to the cottage and beg forgiveness! dozed to the sound of the odd snort as a sow shifted position, squeaks from the babies as they disturbed each other in the warm pile of siblings as they settled down for the night. The last sound he heard before drifting off himself was the gentle shshshfff as a near neighbour passed wind! He smiled to himself and followed her example before sleep overtook him.

When he awoke, his companions were already awake. His mind went back to the previous day's disaster, who could possibly have seen him at Nell's? He had to find out. The only place he had stopped was at Tullagh Mhor. The café.

He knew no-one there and was sure no-one could possibly have known him.

He let himself into the cottage, made some coffee, and left the pot on the stove. After showering, he towelled himself down and dressed into clean working clothes. A piece of toast sufficed for breakfast.

"Hi there Paddy, how are yer doin' son?"

There was a moment's silence before an answer came back.

"Is that you then Sean me old mate?" as Paddy recognised his friend's voice on the phone.

"To be sure. How does it feel to be a free man again? Now listen ...." Sean explained the plan hoping that they would soon be partners in crime, although Sean never did think the supply of potcheen was a criminal act.

"I like it" was the succinct response.

Sean gave Paddy Nellie's phone number and told him to get in touch with her as soon as possible.

Paddy McCormick was familiar with the habits of the police on both sides of the border as his activities with the IRA in the past had taught him how to avoid contact. Sean was aware of this which was why he was sure they would succeed.

"Now Paddy remember, don't call me unless it's absolutely necessary, Rachel must never be aware of any dealings we have I've had to promise her that I won't get personally involved. Are we completely clear on this?"

"That we are Sean, I'll take care of things with Nellie. I'll call her right away and get things moving."

He then rang Nell, informing her that his pal would soon contact her to arrange the first trip.

9

Nell and Paddy hit it off straight away. She was going to enjoy doing business with him and he thought she sounded great on the phone.

The still was fired up and the barley, yeast and sugar measured and were set up to begin the process of "cooking the juice". All was ready for Paddy's visit tomorrow. The illegal brew would improve in quantity, if not in quality!

Thinking about her product brought to Nellie's mind what Mr Butler said in his Irish book which he published in the seventeenth century under the heading 'Irish Moonshine Whiskey'; *'It Enlighteneth ye heart, casts off melancholy, keeps back old age and breaketh ye wind'*.

Quite so!

By the time Paddy arrived at the place two days later, the distillation was in full swing.

"Do ye tink we auter taste it Nell?" Paddy enquired as soon as he smelled the stuff.

"Later lad, it'll have to cool down a bit." she told him.

That evening, over a jar or three of the vicious liquid, they got to know each other. When he could no longer find his glass, Paddy tried to stand up in order to visit the little room. He kept falling over. 'Oh bugger it!' he exclaimed.

As he pulled himself up to a kneeling position he bumped into a large flower pot which kept getting in his way, rather than make another futile attempt at standing up, he relieved himself into this receptacle which obligingly remained in the same place long enough for the procedure to take place.

Nellie didn't notice his behaviour as she was already fast asleep and snoring loudly!

10

Rachel cried herself to sleep the night of the disagreement over the visit to Nellie. She loved her man so much and yet she couldn't help feeling betrayed. Sean hadn't ever shouted at her before, he was a gentle, sensitive individual.   She knew that she would have to come to terms with the situation and she also knew that he was right, something had to be done to improve their financial predicament. It would do Sean no harm though to realise that she couldn't be bullied. He should apologise to her. If he would do so today she'd find a way to put things back to normal. Yes, that's what she'd do.

Sean was full of remorse for upsetting her but he was blowed if he was going to apologise. Now was the time for making a stand. Show her who was boss. He knew that already..... She was!

Life on a pig farm is always pretty hectic, it was not just a case of feeding the creatures and keeping them clean. Being responsible for maintaining hundreds of animals in a healthy and contented condition needed constant attention. The vetinary surgeon was in frequent demand whenever one of the pigs required special treatment.

Occasionally an older sow would have difficuty expelling a part of her litter during farrowing. This would mean having to roll up the sleeves, crouch down or lie on the floor behind the animal then reach inside her to assist the reluctant piglet.

When one of the boars would get agressive towards his keeper it usually meant his tusks had grown too large which gave the animal a superior arrogance, often demonstrated by a gnashing action making sure his keeper could see his intention. A very threatening gesture. To remove this determination by the huge animal it was necessary to saw off his tusks! A job for Mr. Chrichley, the vetinary.

Sean had finished feeding the majority of his charges and was finishing off this task by giving the 'roaming boar' his food pellets which were dispensed by hand from a sack which he carried on his back. This particular animal was the oldest of the four boars kept on the farm. 'Horace,' as he was known, had been delegated to 'look after' the sows and gilts in case they failed to conceive after they had visited one or other of his pals who were kept in the boar house. Horace was given the freedom of the grassy paddock which ajoined the boar house and was free to roam around his patch. Normally fairly docile, the enormous creature would allow Sean to tickle his ears and scratch his back which he obviously enjoyed.

Today was different. Horace stood well away from the entrance to his domain until Sean had reached the centre of the paddock and had begun to trickle a line of feed pellets along the ground. A grateful animal would enjoy gobbling up these delicious offerings ignoring his keeper during the process which was normally the case, even with Horace.

He could obviously sense that Sean was having a bad day and he saw it as his duty to add to this. Lifting his head to give the impression of great height the half ton monster stared at Sean with a beady eye and advanced towards him after issuing a roar of superiority, moving sideways gnashing his yellow teeth and displaying five inch tusks in a very threatening manner he allowed this feeble human who was carrying a whole sack of his favourite grub time to get to the middle of his patch before letting him know that he intended to have the lot. Now!!

Sean was no weakling, nor normally a coward, but the sight of the hungry animal approaching him with ever quickening steps made discretion win comfortably over bravery. The sack was hurriedly dropped as any human being can run much faster without having the burdon of a heavy sack of pig food to slow him down! Three seconds later Sean had leaped over the fence which was topped with barbed wire without, gratefully, a scratch or torn trousers! Horace took his time devouring these pellets, occasionally lifting his head and staring malevolently at Sean.

Mr Crichley arrived early the next morning........

I I

After the trip down to Nellie's and the disturbance this caused to their lives, Sean and Rachel had a serious discussion about how to resolve their personal as well as the business difficulties. They both realised compromise was required. For his part Sean promised never to go behind her back to be involved with her mother. No more clandestine plans. Rachel forgave him again on the strict understanding that this promise would be kept.

It was time to explain to him how she knew that he had lied to her.

"My best friend from school who used to run errands for mum was working in the kitchen of the café you stopped at recognised you from that photo mum has of us both. She wondered why you were on your own and phoned me to see if I was alright."

So that was it. Sean hadn't bothered to see if he recognised anyone at the diner as he was sure this was new territory, it was a lesson in how small the world is. Especially when you really don't want to be noticed. Ah well, experience with hindsight is a wonderfully useless thing! This lesson was taken on board. If it was necessary to avoid being seen in future he would dress up as a chicken!

12

The arrangement Nellie had with Paddy was working out very well.

Rachel was now always informed when contact was made between Sean and her mother. Regular payments in cash were now arriving from her mother as a result. These payments were not going to resolve their problems with Mr. Jones they both knew but they could now enjoy the odd night out and put a little away for emergencies.

The 'hooch' business in the south was progressing quite well after a few teething troubles. Nell had taught Paddy the basics of distillation but his ' feel' for the process wasn't there yet. He was as keen as the proverbial mustard to learn as much as he could so didn't mind the menial tasks associated with the process which she allotted him. Although small in stature Nellie was a strict task-mistress and criticised every small mistake Paddy made. He soon became used to this and didn't mind being admonished. As a result, he learned quickly. His most important job was to measure the ingredients for the mash, this he did with the utmost care as waste would not be tolerated by either of them.

The 'de luxe' version of the spirit was based on barley as the main source of malt, whilst the cheaper version was made with potatoes and peelings from the ones used for cooking their meals. " Waste not, want not" as the saying goes. Nell was a conscientious practitioner!

Paddy had a wide collection of contacts from his days as a 'runner' for the IRA. Many of these had a strong liking for 'a drop of the hard stuff' as it was colloquially known and so the market had grown exponentially. This expansion had produced a distribution challenge, the old methods of transportation could no longer be safely used. Nell and Paddy had spent long hours considering various receptacles, bottles were a possibility but these were difficult to camouflage and could be easily recognised by a diligent Customs officer.

The still was working twenty four hours a day now, this meant shifting hundreds of gallons a week rather than the odd forty. Any large container which might raise suspicion had to be discounted. They were enjoying the success of their partnership too much to put it at risk simply because of the method to be used for transportation. The system they were using at present would have to be changed to allow for shifting industrial quantities of the precious product.

Paddy toured the scrap yards buying up as many petrol tanks from discarded vehicles as he could find which were the right size for his purpose.

So far they had been lucky. Although he had been stopped and searched every time he crossed the border none of the officials had inspected the underside of the vans he was using.

For the first month of his association with Nell Paddy had spent every spare moment underneath one of the 'written-off' vans he had acquired at scrap price which was usually about five Irish punts.

Each vehicle was fitted with two extra petrol tanks which were only accessible from inside the van. A panel in the floor was easily removed once the covering oilcloth was lifted. This system was working very well. Up to a point.

The necessity for secrecy meant that either he or Nellie had to take the vans on the long trip which always took a day to do. Care had to be taken as the state of the roads in the south was getting worse daily. Quite apart from the damage the vehicles were likely to suffer there was a grave danger of the cargo exploding if sparks were generated due to loose gravel flying up from the wheels came in contact with those 'modifications'!

The quality was now so good that it was difficult to tell the difference between Nellies' best and the 'genuine' legal versions and demand was now outstripping supply.

13

On the pig farm the one job which no-one enjoyed, although it never took very long, was to clean the 'wet area' of the fattening houses. These were converted from the sleeping quarters or barracks of the previous occupants, 'other ranks' in RAF parlance. Each of these buildings being about one hundred and twenty feet long and twenty five feet wide with windows set eight feet apart down their length on each side.

At the end of the nastiness with Hitler and Hirohito in nineteen forty six, the airfield and all the buildings were handed over to the civilian authority on a lease. No longer required to dispatch and recover noisy aeroplanes, much to the delight of the civilian population living in close proximity to the place. How they felt with the squealing and stench from pigs since then no one had bothered to ask!

When this place was rented out to Sean's father he set about converting the buildings for their present use. Having been brought up within the farming world he had to be a 'Jack of all trades' as the saying goes, which meant; 'if you want a job doing, get on with it yourself.' The farrowing pens were easy to construct, dividing the building up by building a series of low walls with a steel door to allow humans in and to stop pigs getting out. Simple. The fattening houses though presented more of a challenge as they would have to contain a much larger number of animals which would grow to two hundred pounds in weight during their six months lifetime. To allow this to occur and leave a small profit it was necessary to preserve as much of the body heat generated by the pigs as possible. This was achieved by suspending a false roof over the entire floor area, comprising a framework over which was stretched wire netting. It was then easy to spread a layer of fresh straw which could be easily removed and replaced at intervals to ensure hygiene. This was a very successful form of insulation maintaining the animals body heat by this method improved growth rate, reduced feed cost and left a small margin of profit. The pens themselves were constructed in a similar way to the farrowing pens.

A central passageway was constructed to allow passage of the feed barrow which was an old enamel bath suspended on a steel frame attached to which a pair of wheel-barrow wheels allowed easy movement, very efficient and cheap.

Everything had to be as money was always scarce! The area required for each pen, was fifteen feet in length and eight feet from front to back where a wall had been built three feet from the outside wall into which a steel gate was erected. This gate was to allow the pigs to leave their raised sleeping area and relieve themselves as the need arose in the passageway afforded by this method of construction. This passageway and gate also provided the method of shutting the animals in the sleeping area and allowing access for the lucky individual armed with a large squeegee attached to a long handle to remove the offensive slurry. This handle was extra long to protect the operative from the worst of the 'splash-back' when using it!

When all the animals are shut into the inner area by these doors, it is possible to use the wheeled scales, a cage into which each pig is encouraged to enter in order to be weighed, either willingly or with the assistance of the bottom of a Wellington boot!

This process is repeated every week to determine which of the lucky souls is going for a mystery tour in the cattle truck to the slaughterhouse!

The main reason no one particularly enjoys either cleaning the effluent from these sheds or weighing the screaming objects is the effect the scent has on contact with loved ones or strangers. Chanel No. 5 it is not. Sean, since returning to the place, had taken on the responsibility to carry out these fragrant chores. His 'bird' understood!

Rachel was more than a little grateful for not being required to participate in this duty except on clothes wash-day! Disposal of this pungent material was a problem. Forty pens filled with healthy bowels creates an ocean of the stuff every day. Part of the answer to this was answered by the fortunate siting of an enormous 'septic tank'; a concrete inverted pyramid which measured thirty feet square at the surface, fifteen feet at its base, the whole thing ten feet deep from ground level. Being situated only fifty feet from the nearest fattening house it was a simple job to run a drain pipe from the end of the building into the top of this 'tank'.

Many good ideas look great on paper, some work out as practical solutions and it appeared that this was one of those which may be successful. Initially this was the case. Every time the cleaning was completed many hundreds of gallons of water had to be used to hose down the collection area and assist the whole lot down the pipe into the receptacle. The theory behind this scheme was that the 'solids' would sink to the bottom and the water should run off the top into the overflow pipe which was designed to empty the storm water into a main ditch system. The ditch then ran around the perimeter of the airfield to join the surrounding farmland.   For the first few years the idea ran as planned.

14

"We've had another letter from your friend at the bank."

Rachel announced as they were eating lunchtime sandwiches. It was a beautiful summer's day and they had taken their snack outside to sit and eat it in the little garden Rachel had created.

"What does the little sod want this time?" Sean asked.

"It appears the area manager wants to come and see what we're up to here." She replied.

"Can't the bugger phone or write to us direct? They really ought to have something better to do with their time and our money."

"What do you mean our money?"

"Just have a good look at our statements over this last year and see how much we've had to pay in fees and charges. If they weren't ripping us off with those we wouldn't owe them anything." Rachel chuckled at his outburst.

"I can't see the funny side of this at all." he said.

"I don't think we should ignore him. Besides it might be fun to show him how we clean out the bacon houses!" Rachel responded.

"My God Rache, I think that's a brilliant idea!" he laughed. At that moment he could hear the telephone ringing from its cradle in the porch, he got up from his place next to her on the lawn and slowly walked the short distance to the doorway. After a few minutes he was back. He was not laughing any more.

"What a blinking cheek! The dragoness has just asked for a load of manure for her garden and would I deliver it?" He was referring to Mrs. Jones whom he disliked almost as much as her loathsome husband. Sean knew of course, that it would make their relationship descend to a new low level if he refused the request. The trouble was that Rachel in her usual generous way was always offering the stuff to her friends in the village who always fetched it themselves. One of these must have given the idea of a 'free for all'.

"How many folk are on this gift list of yours Rache ?"

"Half the village I think" she replied.

After the chores for the day were completed Rachel typed their response to the letter received that morning from the bank acceding to the request for their inspector to visit the farm.

During the telephone call Rachel made two days later, it was agreed that the following Wednesday would suit the inspector. It wouldn't be convenient for Sean however, as Wednesday was 'Weighing Day' for the pigs going for slaughter.

15

Nellie was concerned that sooner or later probably sooner, Paddy would get 'caught in the act ' delivering 'The Product'. The need for a new system was now reaching the urgent stage. As it was necessary to cross the border on a regular basis, a more convincing purpose for these visits would have to be found. The money had been rolling in for some time now and the piggy bank could afford to be raided if the use for it could be justified. Now was such a time.

Patrick Morgan Mc Cormick was not an educated man in the historical sense. Raw cunning was a more accurate way to describe his brain power. He had given a lot of thought to the problem ever since Nellie had voiced her fears on the subject of distribution. It had occurred to both of them that whatever method they would use it would have to be observed as an everyday occupation. Tools of a trade as it were. Among the ideas was a bulk liquid tanker for farm milk collections perhaps? Maybe fuel would be more convincing. Either of these were unsuitable as they would be too easy to check up on and have to be able to be observed completing the tasks they were designed for. Any and every form of liquid carrying machine was considered and discarded as it would have to be seen too often by the same official individuals to be credible.

The answer came out of the blue when Paddy was visiting one of his dubious friends to deliver his weekly order of potcheen. The friend lived in the notorious border area of Warren Point in an expensive five bed-roomed house complete with indoor swimming pool, double garage and two luxury cars parked in the driveway. This wealthy friend was 'unemployed' in the legal sense.

The next door neighbour was having an extention built on to the rear of his property. A lorry was standing in the roadway and two men were un-loading a quantity of steel poles which would be attached to the building as scaffolding.

Close inspection whilst chatting to the owner of the house revealed a series of brackets attached to these 'poles' which were also hollow. The germ of an idea was growing in Paddy's overworking brain…..

After Paddy had outlined his plan to Nellie they wasted no time the following day in purchasing five hundred of these tubes from a local scrap dealer who had obtained them for pennies from a builder who had just gone bust.

After giving the inside of the tubes a thorough steam cleaning using a pipe from one of the now numerous stills in the 'factory' some alterations were made using welding equipment. Welding and Paddy were not strangers. Safes without keys needed his skills with this equipment.

The tubes had to have their ends sealed to make them watertight then a hole was drilled in the tubes behind the brackets at each end. These were then tapped to the same guage as central-heating radiator valves. One of these valves would then be screwed into one of these holes with a removable plug fitted in the other one.

This process would have to be repeated on all of the pipes. The workshop was cluttered with the junk associated with welding. Gas bottles on their trolley dominated the centre of the floor with assorted hammers, spanners and steel plating with odd shapes removed from it were scattered across the working area.

The pieces which had been 'modified' were stacked together upright, waiting for removal to the Bedford long wheelbase pick-up truck which was purchased along with the scaffolding. This job was going to take weeks to complete.

Meanwhile Nell was working frantically in the still room mostly on her own.

The mash would have to be prepared when Paddy took the occasional break from his gas bottles. He phoned Sean when the first batch was finished.

"Top of the day it is Sean, we need to get those valves and taps soon I'm almost ready for the change over."

"Are you sure this is going to work Paddy?"

"To be sure" Paddy replied.

"But we could do with some help this end with the production side if we are to keep the customers supplied without interruption."

"Have you got anyone in mind?" Paddy had to admit he hadn't given a thought to introducing another person into the site. Any new addition would have to be thoroughly vetted for trustworthiness. This was a big risk.

"Haven't had time to think about it son."

"Do it Paddy. For God's sake be careful though, we don't want to get our fingers burnt with some greedy prat getting his fingers in the till!"

Sean didn't want to be involved at all now. The farm was beginning to promise a profit. All he needed now was trouble from that quarter. "I'll go into the village this afternoon and get the bits you need."

"Great. I'll let Nell know "

"Oh and Paddy, be very careful." The conversation over, Sean replaced the receiver. Rachel was leaning over the table, she had heard every word of the conversation. Sean could sense her concern and was waiting for the rush of words to hit him. Instead of this she quietly said; "Is there going to be a problem?"

"I don't think so, there shouldn't be anyway. It depends on who he hires."

She detected a feeling of doubt in his words. He had a deep frown. This was not a comfortable situation. If it wasn't for Sean's determination to give her a full blown white wedding, he would not have been involved at all. She had been grateful that he had kept his distance from her Mum's shenanigans with the 'dreadful brew', as she now called the stuff. At least now she was being kept aware of any risks being taken.

Sean had plenty of work to do to take his mind off this problem. First of all the boar's house had to be cleaned out, this was a once a week job and today was the day. Deep in thought as he made his way past the tractor shed and the animal medical store, he realised that if Paddy picked the wrong sort of person a lot could go wrong in his world. For a start Nell could be swindled. Better keep her sweet. There was no use worrying yet. It hadn't happened. He carried on to the boar house.

The visiting lady was young and beautiful and she knew it. Sean watched as she sashayed across the floor. She seemed satisfied that he was interested in her by the way he looked at her. She pretended that she was not particularly interested in him.

Sean knew differently. First it was a gentle sniff behind her ear, then he nuzzled her neck, slowly moving down her body, he whispered sweet nothings before concentrating on her smooth pink belly. *Nothing* was going to stop him now. He was going to have her, totally, or his name wasn't Bradfield Bert the champion Large White boar!

Success again…. Job done, the young gilt was shooed out of his pen into an empty one next door. Soon she would make the aquaintance of 'orrible Orace!' and Sean could get on with cleaning the dirty straw away from the bedding area then forking it into the wheelbarrow which now stood in the entrance. After replacing the soiled straw with half a bale of fresh it was time to move on to the next pen. The cleaning-out process continued for half an hour after which it was time to squeegee the dung passages in the fattening houses. This took a little longer, by which time the lower half of his working clothes were sprayed with a perfume which could only truthfully be described as "minging"!

Paddy had made it clear that he needed the valves and taps fairly quickly. The time was now three thirty, a speedy dash in the old car into the village meant that Sean could get this part of the job done out of the way.

Stopping briefly at the cottage to wash his hands and collect his cheque book he jumped into the car, turned on the ignition and listened to the bark of the engine as the exhaust pipe warned him it had retired. The engine still worked. It moved the car. Another expensive job for another day.

The only parking space available near the hardware store was in the doctor's drive, reserved of course for the use of his patients. It wasn't the first time, and he wasn't the first to use it however time was short, shop closing time was coming up soon.

"Get your digusting vehicle off my damn drive!" was the parting yell from Doctor Fitzgerald as Sean ran down the road. He entered the ironmongers in a breathless state having run all the way from the doctor's. He saw that there were eight or ten people before him waiting to be served. He knew he wouldn't have to wait very long…. One by one these generous folk insisted he should be served before they were…….!

It was always a cunning plan. Pig effluent has to be experienced to be fully appreciated as a weapon when going shopping or visiting when time was short. These jobs should always be tackled within half an hour of executing any task involving close proximity to pig shit !

16

Part of their difficulty, was not having the exclusive use of a base near the border. Without this facility the increased demand itself would cause serious delay in the distribution process.

The lock-up garage they had found half way between Enniskillen and Black Lion was ideal. Handy for the Province and close to the border with the South. This yard was sandwiched between two other business premises. The rear of the property was defended by a fifteen foot high brick wall which was ideal for their purpose. No one could observe the movements inside the yard as these adjoining buildings had no windows overlooking their domain Originally, a jobbing builder had used the place as a store for his equipment, some of his gear was still there and Paddy was able to make good use of it. The four by two timber of which there was at least a couple of hundred feet would be convenient for converting into racks to store the filled tubes.

Paddy decided to start work on preparing for the first consignment the week-end following signing the lease. Sean had suggested that it might be a good idea to start a legitimate business with the scaffolding, doing this would make the whole idea much simpler to organise and probably remove any further risk of discovery by the nosy parker authorities on both sides of the border.

The necessary plans were made to engage a lawyer to see to the legalities, an accountant would also need to be hired.

Both of these professions were not usually included in Sean's business plans as he didn't trust either profession!

It took a week of heated 'persuasion' to convince Nellie that it was the only way to expand the business without arousing suspicion. The more convincing the outfit appeared the less attention would be paid to them all as they went about their 'legitimate' new occupation.

In order to actually set the thing up it would obviously require a little bit of knowledge about the building industry in general and how to erect scaffolding in particular. There was no point in Sean learning how to do this as he had no intention of being involved other than in an advisory capacity, for which Rachel was grateful. Paddy would have to start looking for a suitable candidate to 'front' the new business. The next few weeks were going to be a testing time for the booze brigade!

17

Time was short on the farm at this time also. Rachel and Sean realised that if they were to make any real progress they would have to consider employing some extra help. The ideal candidate would be a strong school leaver.

August was upon them now and the Autumn tasks would have to be attended to. The few acres of the aerodrome that had been allotted to the original lessee was used to grow barley as a supplement to the pig rations they were having to buy from the agricultural merchants in Belfast.

It only took a couple of days to do the ploughing. In the meantime the animals had to be attended to as usual and so a quantity of 'midnight oil' had to be burned . Time had to be put aside also for the official visit of the bank area manager's visit. Rachel and Sean were of a mind in hoping this character would have a modicum of common-sense unlike the odious trainee under manager Jones.

Mr. Fraser the inspector, turned out to be a fairly quiet individual. When he arrived on the yard he was introduced to them by Jones 'the bank' in a very formal manner.

"I would like to introduce my clients, Mr. Sean O'Reilly and Miss Rachel Flanagan . Mr. O'Reilly and Miss Flanagan this is the bank's area inspector, Mr. Fraser."

They shook hands. Mr. Fraser had a good firm hand-shake unlike the revolting limp-fish effort of the dour Jones!

"I would like to see everything you do if we have time." suggested Mr Fraser.

"Of course. Rachel and I are very proud of this place." Sean replied.

During the course of the tour the senior visitor insisted that they should address him as 'Bill' which put the couple at ease instantly. It was clear that a rapport was developing which would exclude the pompous local bank official Jones. The couple didn't know this individual's Christian name and certainly didn't care.

"I think it would be a good idea to lend you some Wellington boots before we go up to the fattening houses Bill." said Rachel.

"No need my dear, I've brought my own." Bill Fraser sat on a bale of straw which had been left outside the farrowing house waiting to be taken inside.

"I wouldn't mind borrowing a pair." said Jones after his senior colleague had finished changing into his well used foot ware.

"Sorry" said Sean, "We don't have any your size." Which was, happily, true!

Mr. Jones was a small individual in physical stature, unlike Bill Fraser who would make a substantial rugby player and probably had been in his youth.

The tour of the farm was completed with Bill Fraser full of complements on what he had seen. The unfortunate bank official was unhappy though, without the protection of a pair of waterproof foot-ware he had accumulated a liberal quantity of free effluent which Rachel noticed with satisfaction, reached almost to his knees! Whilst Bill Fraser went to his car to change into his shoes and remove his overalls Rachel invited the unfortunate bank junior to the bungalow to clean him up as best she could. "If you would like to change into these," she said to him, handing him a pair of Sean's working trousers, which were at least two sizes too large for him.

"I'll just wash those through for you."

Jones didn't thank her, he glowered and snatched the clothes she offered.

The sound of voices coming towards the door made him hurry to the bathroom which was at the end of the hallway. After he had entered the small room he slammed the door behind him and hurriedly changed into the two sizes too large borrowed pair! When the now embarrassed bank official rejoined the group in the small sitting room, they were all sitting down.

"Coffee everyone, or tea?" asked Rachel after carrying a tray stacked with cups, saucers and two pots.

"How very kind of you Rachel" exclaimed Bill.

"I'd love a coffee please."

"How about you Mr Jones?"

"Tea." Was his ignorant response to her polite offering.

After serving them all, the conversation turned to pleasantries.

"Well you two. What are your immediate plans?" asked Bill Fraser.

"Apart from trying to run this place with no help?" Sean said. "No Sean I'm talking about personal plans. You know, holidays, activities away from here. It's important that you enjoy some leisure time."

Jones decided it would be over his dead body to assist these two dumb farmers to make any money for themselves! As long as he was their manager he would keep them on a very short leash. The local big businesses could walk all over him, get whatever financial support they needed but he was damned if these mucky pig farmers were going to!

As they said cheerio to the senior member of the party Sean and Rachel were quite sorry to see him leaving. Before the car left the yard the driver's window was lowered and Bill Fraser said;

"Give me a bell if there's anything I can do to help won't you?" The car sped away leaving the two of them watching after it.

"What a great bloke"

"A very refreshing change" Rachel replied as they turned away and went back to the house.

18

Nellie wasn't happy at all with the situation they were in. All in all things seemed to be getting out of hand. It was one thing putting her trust in Paddy but quite another letting him go on a building site. Nellie understood the need for getting the knowledge of this business, however she liked to be in control of events. All these years she had managed to keep herself in charge of her destiny.

It was time for another 'board meeting'.

"Sean I can't get my head round this problem of the scaffolding business. Things are already too complicated we'll have to find another way."

"Nell we've been over and over this. Its important for you to realise that I cannot help you any more with this. I think its a terrific idea all you've got to do is establish the business. Give the juice a rest for a while and yourself whilst you're at it."

"Hey, I've never had a rest for the last forty years since that no good husband of mine got in with the 'boys' and cleared off to be naughty in Belfast."

"I know that, but I still think it's a good idea. If you concentrate on getting the premises looking like a proper business while Paddy gets himself a job, preferably with one of his mates, to learn the ropes I'm sure it won't take long then you can go flat out to make us a fortune."

"If I'm going to do all the grafting me boyo it's *me* that's going to be rich!"

"O K Nell" was Sean's reply.

19

The phone was ringing when Sean came in from feeding duty.

"Mr O'Reilly?" said the voice in the earpiece.

"Speaking" Sean answered.

"My name is John Forrest, I'm from the council. I'm afraid we have a small problem."

"How can I help?"

"I've had three of your neighbours complaining about a terrible smell coming from the ditch which runs through their properties. They assume it's coming from your operation on the aerodrome."

"I'm sorry to hear that Mr Forrest. Naturally I'll do anything I can sort out any problem arising from our actions. Perhaps you could tell me who has made the complaint so that I could have a word with them personally?"

"I don't think that would be too wise Mr O'Reilly, they were all very agitated about the problem. Left me in no doubt that unless you stop pouring that stuff into the ditch they would be round there with their biggest labourers to, as one of them put, it 'sort you out'."

"OK Mr. Forrest. Would you please just tell them I'll sort it out as soon as I can."

What to do to 'sort this problem' though, it was obvious what had gone wrong, the sheer quantity and regularity of the cleaning process had finally overwhelmed the system. No longer was it just water flowing through the overflow, now the solid stuff was finding it's way to his neighbours. 'I know we wouldn't like it if it was us on the receiving end' he thought. How on earth was he going to dispose of the perishing stuff now?

"Who was on the phone?" Rachel enquired.

"Some bloke from the council."

"What did he want, some free manure?"

"Not really, apparently some of our neighbours are already getting a free sample which they don't really want. It seems the tank for the bacon houses is causing a big problem for them, the solids are now finding their way onto the other farms. We've got to stop putting it down the pipe."

"How are we going to do that?"

"I haven't a clue. Put your thinking cap on girl, we've got to find a way and very soon. That is if you want to keep me in one piece!"

2∅

Nellie and Paddy got down to an evening of serious discussion. An answer had to be found to their difficult distribution problem.

"I can see where Sean is coming from." said Paddy.

"It does make sense you know Nell, if we could only find someone we could trust to do the deliveries we'd be able to carry on as normal, without that I don't see what we can do other than to shut down the operation for a couple of weeks."

"If we do that, we might as well pack up for good." replied Nellie who was in an irritating mood.

"Do you realise how much competition there is and how good some of our competitors are at pinching trade?"

They were going round in circles trying to find the answer. The situation was so frustrating As they were about to quit for the night they were going to force a couple of small ones down to quench their now parched throats. The phone shouted from the hall stand.. . . . . It was Sean.

"I've been giving your little problem some thought." He said.

"How about hiring somebody who is already in the scaffolding trade? He wouldn't need to know anything about the rest of the business would he?"

"Your dear mother always said you had a good brain boyo. Did you hear that Paddy?" Paddy was not in possession of the phone hand piece and so was not involved with the conversation.

"You've got the phone Nell. I'm over here." He said from the other end of the hallway.

"Sean I think you've got it. I'll have a word or two with the lad here. He's bound to know someone like that."

"I think that calls for a drop of the best stuff Paddy." She said as she put the handset back on its cradle. A round or two of Nell's best had Paddy's brain working overtime trying to think of someone he knew who could be described as sixpence short of a bob in the building trade who might be persuaded to work for practically no re-numeration but with a bucketful of promises of a share in the profits of their new enterprise. It was obviously proving too much for his now highly inebriated grey matter to deal with. Nelly recognised the signs and sent him off to bed to sleep off the effects of the hooch. The morning would see a return to relative normality and hopefully, answers.

Breakfast saw a rather subdued Paddy at the table in the small kitchen which doubled as the office. The table was still cluttered with the remnants of the previous evening's indulgence.

There were eight glasses and two large jugs one of which was empty the other still had a drop in its bottom which would have been consumed if Paddy had been able to notice its presence the previous evening.

"O.K. Paddy, let's sort out who you are going to talk to. Whoever it is he must be with us by the end of the week. Have you got someone in mind?" Nellie was getting impatient. She knew that if she didn't bully him, Paddy would carry on procrastinating as he didn't like the idea of another person being involved.

55

Whilst he was now excellent at doing his jobs with the potcheen, he wasn't the most enthusiastic enterpreneur. Ideas didn't come easily to him.

"I'll do some phoning around today I'm sure I can find the right character but I can't guarantee you'll like him."

"You do that son. It doesn't matter whether I like him or not. Just make sure he's the right chap. "The telephone earned it's keep that morning. By the time he'd finished Paddy had three possibilities lined up. He'd also arranged interviews for the next day.

21

Sean had to find an answer for the effluent difficulty urgently.

As he stood next to the exit pipe of the septic tank, he realised that if he could remove the contents and start again the system would have a new lease of life, how to do it though was the problem. It would take weeks to empty the thing by hand and whoever had to do the emptying would permanently pong whilst the process was in progress and probably for weeks afterwards!

He absently gazed over the landscape beyond his own domain. The old control tower from wartime days stood out in its forlorn loneliness. The windows had all gone, so had all the doors but he could almost hear the sound of the aeroplane engines, now long departed. In the grey winter weather which prevailed, the place appeared desolate and abandoned. Sean felt its melancholy as his gaze settled on the concrete area near the septic tank, which had been the floor of one of the hangers where the aircraft had been serviced before setting off to patrol the Western Approaches looking for enemy submarines. The crews would probably have preferred the danger and accompanying fear of one of those patrols over the Atlantic ocean to the idea of cleaning up pig effluent! It all seemed so unreal now.

It suddenly occurred to him that if he could find a pump which could cope with the thick consistency of the slurry he could use this huge concrete pad to act as a sort of evaporation station. It would be a permanent answer to removal of this fragrant problem. Where to find a pump capable of this mammoth task? After making some enquiries via the Belfast Chamber of Trade, he found his answer in Belfast dock-yard.

Harland and Wolf the famous ship-builders had a supply of surplus ex W.D. high capacity pumps, they would be prepared to spare one for the enormous sum of twenty five pounds! Sean rapidly sealed a deal to secure one, all he needed now was a suitable vehicle to transport the enormous piece of equipment across country to the farm. A quick call to Paddy at Kilmona and the Bedford was booked to extend its next trip after delivering its contraband to Enniskillen and pick up the pump from the H & W yard.

The pump had been made in Sweden for use by the Swedish forces and had enjoyed a considerable world-wide market. The U.K. government had bought a large consignment most of which were now surplus to requirement and were lying in Harland and Wolf's yard surplus to requirement. H and W had been putting them in the engine rooms of all the ships they had been building. As competition from Japanese shipyards had decimated the demand for British - built ships making a number of yards redundant, it also meant that a large amount of equipment was now also idle, hence the availability of the pump.

The O'Reilly's were grateful beneficiaries of this situation as these pumps had a huge volume capacity and once primed could move five hundred litres of material per minute. The twin chambers of the pump were large enough to pass solid items the size of a milk bottle. Ideal for its new life. It would soon be put to good use.

22

Paddy grumbled when asked to extend his journey as he was going to have to interview his prospective employees the next day and this new task would take time. It would be good to see Sean again though.

It took him almost three hours to travel the ninety odd miles and the old Bedford was a noisy, smelly old vehicle. It would be great when the business could afford to buy a decent truck. It was dark by the time he reached his destination. Thankfully the Shipyard was still open. Paddy drove through the entrance gates as a group of workers were leaving at the end of their shift. The enormous yellow cranes were in front of him underneath which the early bones of a large vessel were growing up from the bowels of the slipway. To his right were piles of steel girders waiting their turn to becoming part of the ship under construction. On the left of the roadway stood a line of fuel tanks each painted a different colour with a description of the contents. On a board attached to one of the stands was a notice in bright orange, warning of the danger of explosion.

Naked flames and smoking were prohibited near these. This was a place which appeared to have a life of its own, people were everywhere.

A large Victorian building declared itself welcoming as it invited 'all visitors to report here'. Pulling up outside Paddy noticed the door was open and a light was burning inside, he climbed down from his cab and went in. After introducing himself to the young receptionist he explained the reason for his presence; "I have to collect a pump for Mr. O'Reilly."

"Ah yes, I've just had a call from Mr. O'Reilly. He told me to expect you. If you take your truck over to the main handling yard which is next to the first big yellow crane over there." she said pointing to the floodlit yellow monster.

"There's an office there with 'Yard Manager' on the door. Ask for Joe there and he'll sort it out for you."

"Thanks me darlin', see you soon." Paddy drove carefully through the yard until he reached the office.

"Is Joe there?" he shouted after winding down the window of the Bedford.

"Who wants to know?" came the reply from the heavily built man with tatooed arms and head covered by a bright yellow safety helmet.

"Pump for Mr O'Reilly!"

"Right. Pull over there, under that hoist." Paddy carefully negotiated the various machines and objects which sat apparently abandoned in the area and stopped with the empty deck of the vehicle sitting directly under a large crate which swung gently above. After only a few seconds the crate slowly sank until its weight made itself known to the waiting truck which settled down heavily on its springs. Half a ton of cast steel machine was now on its way to solving the slurry problem on the farm. Sean was patiently awaiting the arrival which was late at night, too late for Paddy to start his return journey to Enniskillen but not too late for a few drops of the hard stuff he had brought with him which he shared with his overnight hosts. Rachel made supper for him. Irish stew, one of Paddy's favourite dishes was consumed with relish before he settled himself down on the old sofa-bed prepared for him by Rachel.

The following morning they had the task of un-loading the heavy pump in its crate alongside the septic tank. This turned out to be somewhat complicated as the load had moved during its journey, even though it had been carefully lashed to the sides of the Bedford. How to un-jam half a ton of machinery without damaging it? Sean scratched his head in frustration. A crane would have been handy. Whatever they did, whichever way they pulled or pushed, the thing wouldn't shift. Levers didn't work, jerking the lorry was just as un-successful.

Eventually it was decided that they would have to employ the Fire Brigade with their heavy lifting gear. This turned out to be the solution albeit a very expensive one as the chief fire officer made clear;

"Our equipment and personnel are there for fighting fires or attending emergencies not assisting farmers with jammed lorry loads!" The bill came to slightly more than the total cost of the pump and the lorry's fuel. Having finally sited the pump and connecting a large bore fire-hose to the inlet connection with a long length of similar diameter to the exit flange it was time for the turning on ceremony.

The fire crew were interested to observe as pumps were stock in trade to them, stood close to the machine examining it. Rachel, Sean and Paddy were assembled with the fire crew as Sean started the engine to begin the process of emptying the offending stuff out to the surrounding concrete area. The engine spang into life with a steady diesel thumping sound. The valve gear was engaged…. Nothing. No sign of liquid movement, just the diesel engine attempting to persuade its sucking machine partner to do the job it was designed for. Sean tried repeatedly to get the thing going without success. The pipe into the slurry was checked again and again. No luck.One of the firemen suggested that the instruction book should be studied. What a good idea! The first line in the book gave them a clue. . . . 'First. PRIME THE CHAMBERS. TO DO THIS, POUR SUFFICIENT FLUID INTO EACH OF THESE etcetera….' The instructions went into details of operating the pump.

The group now stood close together discussing the merits of reading the instructions. Meanwhile Sean primed these chambers using an old tin can he had found outside the fattening houses. He then threw the lever to start the pumping action. For a second, the pump made a loud gurgling sound, followed rapidly by a tortured thrashing about of the exit hose…...What happened next came as a surprise to the group. A nasty, wet smelly surprise! as the hose thrashed about discharging its contents in a solid stream, it sprayed them all until they were unrecognisable from each other! Sean did his best to turn this now living snake off as quickly as possible shaking with laughter and sludge as he did so. No one else could see the humorous side of their situation.

The Chief Fire Officer was certainly not amused! In fact he was so annoyed he told Sean that the clean up of his men, their clothes and equipment was going to 'cost a bomb' and he expected to be reimbursed. It was obvious that the effluent problem was solved.

After the slurry solution had been found the farm itself went from strength to strength, but the couple's financial situation had hardly improved. It needed some radical thinking to see how best to diversify. Strangely the answer came by accident.

23

Now, five years after the solution was found for the disposal of waste from the fattening houses a new, valuable product was being packaged and sold to garden centres and the individual public at large. The massive quantity of effluent leaving the fattening houses was virtually unmanageable as fertilizer on its own. Sean had decided to try and 'clean up' the area by mixing the contents of the straw-laden middens from the farrowing houses and other yards which had built up over the years. The resulting mix was tested by Mrs. Jones and other village worthies and given an enthusiastic endorsement. The examples of its efficacy were displayed at the annual village root show. The blemish free, super sized potatoes, marrow, chrysanthemums and other prize winning flowers and vegetables, which had benefitted from being fed with Mick's Mix as it had now been euphemistically christened, were on show for all to see. Thereby justifying the price of five pounds a trailer load the O'Reillys now charged.

Now that 'Magi-Mix' was in demand locally it was giving a healthy boost to the cash flow of the farm. Sean and Rachel agreed that it made sense to develop a separate business to sell the product commercially. To do so it would be necessary to 'package' the material in an attractive way which of course, meant researching the availability of machinery required to do this. A call to the Belfast Chamber of Trade gave them the names and telephone numbers of two international companies who specialised in this area. After lengthy consultation with the sales directors of these companies it was decided which of these firms could produce the appropriate equipment. The price quoted frightened them however.

"I'll have to go and see the idiot Jones again and try and talk some sense into him. I hope to God he will be able to understand the obvious sense of this scheme." Sean said to Rachel.

"I don't know about that. I expect he'll be just the same." She replied.

"If he treats me like a child this time, I'll damn well behave like one and thump him!"

"Oh yes; that would really make him behave…I don't think." Rachel responded.

"Tell you what, before you do anything stupid why don't you give Bill Fraser a ring? He did say to keep in touch didn't he?"

"I'd completely forgotten about him. I might just do that."

Sean and Bill had a pleasant conversation and it seemed to Sean that Bill was in total agreement with both the idea itself and the way to promote it. A call to the bank to make another appointment with their Nemesis was made. Jones was now the couple's official bank manager following his long awaited promotion.

"Next Monday two thirty. OK I'll be there." Sean said to Jones' secretary in response to her instruction. At least this time he could use the strength of Bill Fraser's support. The little twerp surely couldn't refuse the loan this time, even if the terms of the loan were not the most favourable as he was certain they wouldn't be. The couple knew it would be another unpleasant interlude. Ah well…....

There was a knock on the door as they were finishing lunch. Standing outside was a man who was fidgeting nervously with the brief-case he was carrying.

He was quite smartly dressed in a dark grey suit over a white shirt, with a light blue tie on which was embroidered a logo in gold of a harp beneath which were the letters; N.F.U.I. He also wore a cap of indeterminate colour. He removed his hat as he introduced himself to Rachel who had opened the door to him.

"Good afternoon Madam, I'm sorry to disturb you. My name is Paul Moffatt, I represent the National Farmers' Union of Ireland. I would like to introduce you to a great investment opportunity. May I come in and talk to you about it?"

"I suppose so, as you're here." She said, feeling generous to such a polite young man.

"Who is it?" Sean's voice said from the kitchen.

"It's a chap from the N.F.U. Sean. Wants to talk to us about some kind of investment." As there was nothing pressing to do at that moment Sean agreed to give Mr. Moffatt a few minutes of his 'valuable' time. Paul Moffatt eloquently went through his sales patter explaining that for five quid a month the life insurance package would be worth many thousands of pounds on maturity, when Sean reached sixty five years of age, seemingly an eternity away in the distance.

"Looks great on paper Mr Moffatt. Give us a day or two to think it over. I am interested"

Later, a very happy insurance salesman departed convinced that another sale was done.

"Are we really interested in all that?" Rachel asked.

"Well if he's half way right it'll come in handy and we can afford a fiver a month can't we?" Rachel smiled and agreed.

"I think I'll give Nell or Paddy a bell and find out how they're getting on." It had been some time since he had spoken to either of them and thought it would be interesting to see if the business was still doing well.

24

Paddy had made an excellent choice with Mickey Kelly as building 'advisor'. Mickey was a crafty little sod who knew how to 'work the system ' almost as well as Paddy himself.

Like so many from his home town he was fatherless, although not because his ma was free with her favours outside marriage but because his father had been killed by the security forces. He had been a popular boy at school always laughing and joking as though he hadn't a care in the world. In fact he was really a serious individual and realised that to succeed in the cruel environment he was born into he would have to be able to make people laugh. He would also have to be street-wise. The latter was demonstrated to Paddy during his interview; when asked where he lived he said: 'During the day I live where I am at the time. At night I live in the bar where I'm drinking. After that I don't really know, or care. In the morning I live where I am at the time' His answer was understood by Paddy who had experienced a similar existence in his own past.

During his years as a builders' labourer, Mickey had learned all there was to know about building houses and a considerable amount about commercial 'sheds,'.. . . . . factories and large stores. He also knew how to handle the union extremists when they were agitating. The scaffolding operation was explained to him leaving out of course, the primary use of the steel tubes, secrecy about their true function had to be jealously guarded.

This was his first job as an executive. The guy in charge.

Paddy explained to Mickey that the tubes with a band of black paint around the end of them were not to be used 'on the job'. No questions to be asked as they would not be answered. Mickey naturally knew better than to demand knowledge outside his own responsibilities.

He was just very happy to be 'the man in charge'. An important position for a person from his back-ground and he was determined to make the most of this situation.

He quickly began to organise the yard, a comprehensive storage system for all the scaffolding components, separating the tubes with the black rings painted on them from the main stock of tubes which he would be using on the job.

Paddy was quick to appreciate his new employee and offered his acknowledgement of the lad's efficiency.

"I'll be dropping in fairly regularly to keep on top of this new enterprise Mickey. It'll probably be outside business hours so don't worry if I'm already here when you arrive for work."

It had been necessary to tell Mickey this in order to be able to do the 'shuffling' of the pipes in and out of the yard without causing the lad to be suspicious of his nefarious activity.

Time to nip down to Kilmona and give Nellie the good news of the successful placing of the final pieces of the jigsaw allowing them to continue 'trading!

25

One minute it was Tuesday, a very busy day on the farm. The next it was bank-visiting day. Wednesday arrived without making a fuss. Sean did the vital chores, feeding, cleaning out, putting 'ripe' sows to the boars to start the cycle again. Once more showered and smartly presented he made his way to the bank and tapped on the manager's door. He was kept waiting outside the office for a full two minutes before the pompous official invited him in.

"Good morning Mr Jones, it's so good of you to see me again at such short notice." Sean stated facetiously. A grunt was returned by the man sitting at his desk opposite. The rude response was ignored by Sean. He was sure that this time he would get what he wanted. A chance to provide the bank with a stack of profit over the term of the loan as yet not granted. After laying out the plan of the new enterprise in great detail with carefully calculated projections including expected profit over its first six months of operation. The figures showed that the return on capital would be in excess of two hundred per cent above the value of the loan. Jones showed no interest whatever in the presentation. His mind was made up. After the humiliation of the visit to the farm with his superior as a spectator there would be definitely no loan!

26

Nellie and Paddy were doing a great trade with the hooch. So good in fact that demand now well outstripped supply. The Bedford was now doing a daily return trip to Kilmona for fresh supplies. It was hard to understand why this was happening so suddenly. "Paddy, do you think you could ask a few of the regulars why they are drinking so much more these days?"

"Yeah. O.K. Nell, will do."

"If we know the reason maybe we could open up in the south here."

"I don't know about that. There's a hell of a lot of established competition down here isn't there?"

"That maybe so lad, the fact remains we are now doing three times as much as this time last year. I checked the books last night. I can't understand it for the life of me"

"Do you think we will be *able* to produce any more. The stills are already working night and day. We don't have the room to set up any more of them do we?"

"Just try and find out why they love the stuff so much then we can decide what to do."

After the last of the tubes had been filled Paddy took a large night-cap and went to bed. Early the following morning after a hasty breakfast of his usual fried bacon, two eggs, three sausages, half a large tin of baked beans, tomato and fried bread plus two cups of coffee to wash it all down he grabbed his jacket and climbed into the cab of the Bedford. Nellie waved as he drove away from the house and started on his way to the yard up north. She insisted on feeding her valuable colleague she reckoned that a good, solid breakfast would save him having to stop anywhere for lunch saving valuable time. The 'milk-run' as Paddy liked to call it was going nicely, he was humming to himself an old tune that he remembered from his childhood. He couldn't remember all the words his father used to sing but the melody had stayed with him through the years and it brought back vague memories of his long lost dad.

He didn't notice the Garda vehicle flashing its headlights and blues in his mirror. He suffered quite a jolt when the siren was turned on. This brought him back to reality and he immediately pulled in to the side of the road. 'Now what the devil have they done this for?' he thought as the vehicle came to a stop.

"Hello Paddy me lad." The Sergeant said as Paddy rolled down the window.

"I haven't seen you for a long time. What mischief will you be up to now I wonder?"

"Well now if it isn't me favourite copper?" He returned, trying not to appear nervous.

"It's come to our attention that someone is making some pretty good potcheen in this area. I don't suppose you would know anything about it would you Paddy?"

"How would I know anything about something as despicable as that indeed?"

"Now why would I expect any other kind of answer than that?"

Paddy looked down at the sergeant whom he had known for many years. He knew him well, because he had been arrested by him on a few occasions in the past for minor crimes.

"Just step down now lad. I want to have a good look at this load of junk you have in the back. More specifically I want to look *under* it all. Just to make sure you're not carrying anything that you shouldn't be."

"What a nasty suspicious mind you have officer. You know I did time in prison. Why would I risk going back there?"

"Paddy old son, I'm a very trusting man so I am. Just you ask the Father next time you're in Church! Have you got your driving licence with you?"

"To be sure Officer. I wouldn't travel without it." The statement was true.

There was no point in tempting fate. If everything else was above board, why should anyone suspect there might be criminal activity going on?

A thorough search was made by the Sergeant and his two companions. A number of the filled tubes were removed and thrown on the grass verge. One officer was on his back under the lorry examining every dirty nook and cranny. Paddy was enjoying a certain satisfaction knowing they were not going to find any incriminating evidence. That was until the sergeant noticed a line of liquid dripping out of one of the pipes…..

"No that's strange. It hasn't rained for days. Let's have a closer look at these pipes!" suggested the sergeant.

27

Sean arrived back at the farm in a state of fury the like of which Rachel had never seen.

"Don't tell me," she said, "He won't lend us the cash will he?"

"No! The silly little bugger won't." He replied with growing anger and frustration. " He wouldn't even listen. How are we going to get the silly twerp to see reason?"

"Why don't you give Bill a ring and tell him what's happened?"

"You know me Rache. I like to fight my own battles, but I have to admit I cannot fight an unwinable war, that idiot must really hate us. I'm damned if I know what we've done over the years to upset him."

"Well I still think you should give Bill Fraser a ring and explain the problem to him, he should be able to batter some sense into the man."

"OK You win. I'll give Bill a tinkle some time, I am too annoyed to talk with him now."

The farm was now demanding more attention than ever. It was imperative that extra help was found. It came in the shape of a pretty young school leaver, her name was Sheila Ferguson.

Sheila was the daughter of the local butcher. Rachel and Sean had known the family ever since Sean had arrived back on the farm in nineteen sixty one.

Many a Sunday joint of beef or lamb had come from their shop. Sam Ferguson enjoyed a highly respected reputation for most of his meat the notable exception had been the pig products he sold. The pork and bacon he offered to his customers was of poor quality, there was more fat on these products than a hippo's backside according to Sean.

"Where on earth do you get your pork and bacon from Sam?" queried Rachel when buying a chicken from him one day.

"I have to get it from the slaughterhouse, I try to pick the best they have but to be honest Rachel, none of it is much good. The trouble is all the pig meat comes from third grade swill fed animals from the local farms which the company says it has to sell here in Ireland. All the good stuff like yours is exported for the English market.

Makes sense to them I suppose but doesn't do our business any good at all."

"I can fix that for you if you like, I'll get Sean to speak to the manager at the slaughter-house, I'm sure he'll be able to divert some of the best pig meat you've ever tasted" A quick phone call was all it took for Sean to secure the 'right stuff' for Sam Ferguson (and some favouritism with good cuts of meat for Rachel Flanagan!).

"Next time you're at the abattoir, tell the slaughter man to give you a flitch with the code number H 41 B. That's our code which we tattoo on the sides of each animal before it leaves our place."

"Thanks Sean, I'll do that." Sam replied with gratitude. When the meat arrived the Ferguson family tried out their purchase only to find they needed second helpings of the delicious bacon. Sunday would see a large joint of pork which had also been purchased ravenously devoured by all!

Sheila turned out to be a willing and very reliable helper on the farm.

With the notable exception of the bank and its spiteful manager things were looking better than they had ever done.

Numbers of triple grade 'A' carcases being sold for the top price, average numbers of piglets being born to the sows running at nine point two....

Excellent. Sean could now at last, suggest to that woman he adored that it was time to 'Set the Date'. This evening he would do just that!

28

The sergeant lifted the tube which appeared to be leaking. He couldn't understand how the pipe could hold water when it was stacked in the truck at an angle. Surely the water would have drained out of it long ago.

"Well now me boyo, something doesn't seem to add up here."

"I don't follow," said Paddy, feeling the situation getting out of control.

"I'm sure you *do* son." The officer slowly bent down to run his finger through the liquid which trickled out of the damaged valve. Putting his wet finger under his nose giving it a good sniff.

"Well now would you believe it. I think the leprechauns have been using your scaffolding to store their liquid refreshment!" The sergeant's face had developed a huge grin of satisfaction. He had found the elusive potcheen smugglers. He had to hand it to them, it was a brilliant scheme which had obviously been working well for years! The two constables who had accompanied Sergeant Murphy hadn't heard the exchange between the two men.

"Gotcher, Paddy old mate I think we've got a lot to talk about."

The sergeant was so pleased with this discovery, it would surely be a certain stepping stone to promotion. This evening he would celebrate with his superiors. Take this golden opportunity to brag about his detective skills.

29

Sean came into the kitchen and told Rachel to get her Sunday best outfit on. They were going out to dinner that evening. She didn't argue. It had been months since they had been out together and that was only for a quick lunch.

The bath was steaming hot. The scented oil she had put in it was pure luxury. She had been given the expensive liquid as a Christmas present; the only time of year when she and her man received expensive gifts from each other, frugality never allowed for extravagances like this normally.

Rachel sensed that this evening was going to be something *special*.

She was pleased to see Sean had shaved and dressed in his Sunday best clothes, he had even used his aftershave, another Christmas gift!

"Jones the bank never got a sniff of your perfume Sean. How come I'm being treated. What are you up to?"

"Shut up woman. I'm trying the romantic bit!"

"Keep going, its working." she laughed.

"What's the occasion anyway?" she persisted. Sean ignored the question and just said;

"Your carriage awaits madam," holding the rusty, battered door of the ancient Austin open for her.

She gathered her best frock around her as she stepped as carefully as possible into the old car. Sean had thoughtfully covered the passenger seat with a clean blanket to protect her from years of farm dirt to avoid damaging her ensemble!

3∅

Sergeant Roger Casey wore a satisfied grin as he stood and looked at the unfortunate Paddy, who felt very uncomfortable. All he could do now was try and bluff his way through.

"I don't know anything about that stuff officer. When I catch the cheeky sod who put it on my truck I'll break his ruddy arm!"

"That kind of language isn't going to help you. You'd best come clean and tell me the whole story?" Paddy knew he was caught red handed but continued to deny any involvement. The two constables who were with Roger Casey had gone back to the car. They had heard nothing of this confrontation.

"Where do you keep this heap McCormick."

"Back at the depot on the road from Black Lion to Enniskillen. The entrance is half a mile past the golf club, you know the one?"

"It's nearly dark now so we'll take it there now." The officer suggested Paddy should lead the way.

"We'll lock the yard and I'll be back at ten o'clock in the morning. I've got to get this mobile scrap-yard off the road. *Do not touch the evidence. I'll inspect all the tubes on it tomorrow.* Understand ?"

"Of course officer Casey. Early it is."

Casey watched as Paddy locked the gate then took the keys off him and just to make sure the evidence couldn't be tampered with overnight he added an extra padlock and chain through the gate's bars before setting off to enjoy his triumphant evening drinking session with his colleagues, he couldn't get there quick enough!

Much later that evening Paddy jumped into the old Land-Rover he was using and put his foot hard down on the accelerator to bring the speed up to a breathtaking forty three miles per hour, he had to get there as quickly as possible….. A cunning plan had begun to form.

Sergeant Casey didn't realise that Paddy could access the yard over the neighbouring rooftop!

It was two in the morning when the Land-rover came to a standstill outside the main store shed, Paddy scrambled out of the cab, leant the ladder he had brought with him against the neighbouring wall and climbed over the roof then dropped down into the yard. He opened the entrance to where the rack of scaffolding was standing, jacket off, sleeves rolled up, the long night and cunning plan began…..

Spot on six o'clock the next morning the Garda vehicle pulled up at the yard. A single figure climbed out of the highly polished official police car. Sergeant Roger Casey kept his promise to his unfortunate prey, it was early, not the ordered ten o'clock. Paddy suspected this would be the crafty officer's plan. Casey used the keys confiscated from his suspect and un-locked the gate, retrieved his own lock and chain and unhurriedly examined the perimeter of the property leaving no stone, stick or piece of junk untouched.

Paddy was in no hurry to go to work that morning. He knew his adversary would be true to his word and was not surprised to see the official vehicle at rest outside his property.

"Top o' the mornin to yez sergeant." Paddy saluted when he came across the policeman going through the rubbish bin at the rear of the building.

"Let's have a look at the evidence then"

"I bet you wouldn't trust your own granny with your washing Sergeant!"

"You haven't interfered with it have you? If you have I'll chuck the library at you!"

"Of course not sir how could I? You had my keys and I haven't done anything wrong so why would I?" Paddy returned with a pained, innocent expression on his face. An intensive search was about to get underway when the telephone was telling them that someone wanted to have a conversation. Paddy casually strolled over to where the phone hung on the wall.

"Hello… Yes, he is speaking to you."

Mickey Kelly had also noticed the official car outside the yard as he was arriving for work. Pretending to be a client wanting to talk business he had dialled the office from the public call box near the yard to see if Paddy was inside and find out what the devil was going on. Because of the officer's close presence Paddy was unable to say exactly what was going on but he wanted to keep Mickey, who was totally ignorant of the real nature of the business, out of the way in case embarrassing questions were directed at him. Mickey's innocent truthful answers could scupper them all.

"Well you'll probably find him at the new site at Lougher sir. If you go over there he'll be able to help you." Mickey although not the most efficient spanner in the toolbox realised that Paddy wanted to keep him away from this particular action, took the hint told Paddy he understood and took the day off work and went fishing…

It was lunchtime before all of the tubes from the back of the truck had been lifted off and scrutinised by the suspicious officer, the only one offering any evidence was the one with the damaged valve. Paddy realised that he couldn't convince anyone having already discovered the guilty secret of the presence of alcohol that there was 'nothing to find'. Better to make sure that this one was rediscovered.

Through the night Paddy had removed the precious cargo-laden pipes and replaced them with unadulterated normal tubes in similar condition to those he had removed, all he had to do now was pray that the inspection wouldn't include the huge stack of scaffolding which included of course, the ones from the lorry!

Luck went with him. When the search concluded with no further discovery, the only evidence available to Roger Casey was the smell of the stuff on the end of one scaffolding tube the contents of which had long since drained away! Not enough evidence to take to court and expect a conviction. The officer knew that he had been fooled and he wasn't at all pleased.

"I know you're at it McCormick. I know you are supplying half the British army with the stuff, for all I know probably the other half as well!

When a very angry Casey finally left, Paddy went into Black Lion for some lunch. A ham sandwich, piece of hard cheese with pickle and a pint of Ireland's best Guinness. Afterwards he rang Nellie and told her the whole story.

"Saints be praised son. I'm glad you fooled him this time. You do realise though, we'll have to find another way to shift it now?"

"I really don't think we'll have to Nell, the guy's obviously like the rest of the Garda. Thick as they come!"

"I've had a word with someone I know at the registry." Nellie told him, changing the subject

"She says I could get my licence to make the stuff legally. If I *can* get it, we could set up a proper factory in Dublin."

"There would be no fun then Nell. I don't think I'd like that!" Paddy expostulated.

31

Rachel and Sean were enjoying the best meal either of them had ever experienced. The Restaurant was the best in town, red and gold patterned paper lined the walls. There were three chandeliers equally spaced along its length and the tables were covered with crisply ironed cloths. Each table had a cut-glass candlestick in its centre. There was a leather-bound menu and separate wine list placed on each one. Some of the tables were large enough for four or six people, there were also four tables set in booths round the edge of the room.

It was in one of these intimate cubicles they sat gazing at each other through the dim flickering light of the candle. They had agreed that they wouldn't 'talk shop' this evening. The head waiter entered the booth and poured a drop of wine into Sean's glass for him to test for corkage, or some such thing. Sean knew nothing about wine beyond the fact that it often tasted quite good with food. He went through the accepted action first sniffing, then after swilling the red liquid round his glass a few times took a sip.

"Aye that's nice stuff so it is" he said. The waiter took Rachel's glass and filled it to the required level before topping up Sean's. The menu was scrutinised. Rachel noticed the price of each course and thought she could feed them both for at least a week for the cost of one portion! They made their choice from the menu and sat listening to the soft music which swam over them as they sat there. The food arrived and was a delicious experience enjoyed immensely by them both.

"Now will you tell me the reason for this extravagance please Sean." Rachel pleaded. He reached into his jacket pocket and opened his hand to reveal a small black box. Rachel realised immediately what it was. A tear escaped and trickled down her beautiful face which in the low light was breathtaking to Sean. He realised that she knew what was coming but carried on just the same with his carefully rehearsed proposal of marriage. Sean had a catch in his voice when the words came out. He reached over the table and took her hand. As they gazed into each other's eyes he said;

"I've loved you since we were children, as you know . Being a complete romantic I've often dreamt of this moment. I want to sweep you off your size tens! Will you be willing to help me clean out the boar house after marrying me?" Now the smile on her face developed into that wonderful infectious laugh that everyone who knew her enjoyed, the tears came down now like two fairy waterfalls.

"Oh yes Sean you know I will, but I think I can take a rain-check on the boar house!" They laughed until they were both crying like a couple of small children.

32

Business as usual continued between Kilmona and Black Lion. The narrow escape with the law shook them. Paddy was sworn to secrecy by Nellie.

"Don't mention any of it to Sean. If you do he and Rachel will go into orbit!"

"I think we'll have a little holiday Paddy. That pig Casey will be watching us for a while. Make sure you are out and about with a truck-load of the normal scaffolding. With luck he'll stop you a few times."

"Maybe, if he searches us a couple of times, we can get him done for harassment?" Paddy replied.

"Now you're thinking wicked thoughts Paddy, I like it." The more they thought about it the more they liked the idea of screwing the interfering copper. The plan was easy to operate as their scaffolding business was a very profitable one, constant demand meant daily deliveries both sides of the border.

Mickey was kept very busy for the next two months until one day, just after he left the yard with a very big load of tubes he was stopped by the Garda.

Time for celebration in Kilmona. Paddy lifted his hooch laden glass in a toast to the unsuspecting Roger Casey. Nellie raised hers to touch the offered one. It was important if their plan was to work, that an immediate protest was made to the Chief of Police in Co Cork. It would probably be almost totally ignored, it would take three or four separate occasions before these protests would be acted upon, still this was the satisfactory start.

33

Mickey Kelly was annoyed at being disturbed whilst doing his legitimate job and he was loudly vociferous to the officer who had stopped him and examined every piece of scaffolding on the back of the Bedford. What the hell did he expect to find inside a load of pipes? Whiskey? Paddy chuckled at that one! If only the lad knew. It became necessary to revert to their original transportation methods temporarily, it also meant a deal of midnight oil would have to burn if all their customers were to be kept supplied. Nellie was curious to know why their product was so popular, it couldn't have just been the price which admittedly was very competitive. There had to be more to it than that.

"Paddy do you know any of these people intimately, I mean well enough to find out why they buy so much of it?"

"Nell I know all of them like that. It's me personal charm so it is that does it!"

"Of course, why didn't I think of that... Seriously, we need to find out if ours is different to all the others, if we are doing something with the blending I need to know."

"I'll see to it next time I'm in Enniskillen, there's a couple of punters there who will tell it to me straight." Nellie was determined to legitimise her 'moonshine' and if there was a special ingredient which made that difference she would need to know what it was .

34

Their future fortune depended on setting up the packaging plant for their 'Magi-Mix' fertiliser. There must be a way of getting that moron at the bank to understand the logic, both for the couple and the bank. A golden opportunity was being jeopardised by one ignorant man. The trouble was what could be done about it? Sean was mulling the problem over in his mind as he did the morning chores. Damn the man!

The last pen was finished when Rachel called him from the door.

"Come on handsome fiance. Coffee up!" They were sitting outside the cottage drinking their coffee, it was another gorgeous May day. Apart from a baby cumulus cloud the sky was totally undisturbed.

"A penny for them?" Rachel whispered.

"Not worth a great deal more," was the quiet response.

"You're worried about not getting the loan aren't you,?

"Yes of course but that's not what I was thinking about. Well not directly anyway."

"Give." She said.

"Well I was thinking about giving Bill Fraser a ring, see if he can shift the idiot. If we could just get the job under way by the end of next month we'll have time to get a proper honeymoon organised."

"Ring him now. Please Sean."

Sean found Bill's phone number where he had left it under the bedside clock and dialled the number. It took six rings before a female voice answered.

Sean told her who he was and asked to speak to Bill.

"Just a moment. What did you say your name was,? oh yes." Sean heard Bill's name being called , after what seemed like half an hour a familiar voice said;

"Hello Sean how nice to hear you." As it had been some time since the inspection Sean didn't know how Bill would react to a phone call out of the blue like this.

"What can I do for you?" It was a friendly response which was so different to his junior colleague's taciturn effort.

"I have a problem I would like to run past you Bill. I would appreciate your advice."

"Sure Sean, if I can be of any help I would be delighted."

"Could we have lunch sometime soon, maybe at the pub in the village?, unless you'd prefer me to come over to see you there.?"

"No. The pub's fine. When?"

"As soon as." Sean answered.

"How about tomorrow then, about one thirty do?"

"That's great Bill. I'd like Rachel to join us if that's OK with you "

"I would have been very disappointed if she didn't!"

"Thanks a bunch. See you tomorrow then." Bill Fraser was as good as his word. Rachel heard the car arrive at a couple of minutes after the one o'clock news began on the radio. They were ready to go as Bill arrived and they went towards the decrepit Austin.

"Hi folks. You don't think I'm going to join you in that relic do you?" Bill said, laughing as he did so. The three of them arrived at the pub in Bill's new Rover car which embarrassed Sean and delighted Rachel as comfortable travel was a novelty!

Rachel chose a table near a window through which sunlight was streaming.

Sean went to the bar to order the drinks. By the time he returned with them Rachel had chosen a seat which allowed the sun's rays to settle on her left hand as it rested on the table. Her diamond sparkled like a dozen fireworks leaving multi-coloured lights glittering on the tablecloth. Bill noticed the pattern dancing on the white linen .

"Don't tell me... You want me to be a bridesmaid?"

Rachel's cheeks coloured up with embarrassment. Sean and Bill chuckled at her discomfort. After ordering their lunch Sean began to explain to his friend the reason for the meeting. Having described the new venture and how it came about Sean told Bill about the problem they were having getting a loan from the bank. Rachel interjected by saying in a loud voice;

"That nasty vindictive little horror hasn't got the brain of a snail, and is twice as ugly!" Bill and Sean looked at each other in surprise at the outburst.

"Steady on love, it isn't going to help. Bill doesn't want to hear his colleague being insulted does he?" Bill Fraser didn't respond, he just looked uncomfortable. After a few awkward minutes he said;

"I can't approach him directly. For me to interfere in his area of business is just not possible. However I think I know someone who can….."

"I don't want to have to change banks Bill. It would be too awkward to travel to Belfast every time I want something like this."

"I understand Sean. Leave this with me. It might take a week or so."

By this time Rachel had returned to her attractive normal self. "When is the big day?" asked Bill changing the subject. He realised that the relationship between these two and his bank was nearing rock bottom. It was obvious that the new business idea was solid. A great deal of money was waiting to be made and the bank would obviously benefit from it. Mountains would be shifted if necessary.

"We're hoping to have the ceremony next spring if the Church can fit us in. You and your wife will be getting an invitation of course."

"Jane and I will look forward to that." As Bill drove them back to the farm after their meeting he told them not to worry as he felt sure that things at the bank would soon alter.

35

Things were moving in Kilmona. They had been going flat out with distilling the potcheen until they decided to change back to the original delivery system. Suddenly the sales slowed down to requiring only one delivery a week instead of the frenetic daily round trips. This was curious, it was also annoying as far as Nellie was concerned. She had to find out why. Paddy had spoken to many of their customers to try to establish the reason for the popularity of their particular brand of hooch, one after another came up with the same answer, it tasted the same as everyone else's. There was, however, a big difference in its effect on the body. Consumption of potcheen which was between twelve and fifteen per cent alcohol content averaged one bottle per person per day. Nellie's stuff was different, a sniff of the stuff was equivalent to a generous glassful, a small shot would send the average drinker into orbit! Blind drunk!

Something had caused an enormous increase in the alcohol content. When Paddy reported this to Nellie she was mystified, there was absolutely no difference in the process of making the stuff to the way she had always made it.

Perhaps the barley was the cause? The first thing to do was to test the latest brew which she did. Thirteen point four per cent... absolutely normal. This truly was a mystery. Why though, had the sales suddenly fallen? What was different now?

Paddy came up with the answer when he realised that they were no longer using the scaffolding tubes for delivery.

"Have we any in tubes now?" queried Nellie.

"I think so, I'll pop into the yard tomorrow and see." Paddy replied. The next day he went up to the yard early and found two full ones, from these he filled two bottles to return to the distillery. After testing these they were astonished to find an alcohol reading of ninety eight per cent. *Ninety eight percent*!! Wow!

"No wonder the buggers like our stuff. We've been selling it far too cheap!" exclaimed Nellie.

"For sure" added Paddy. It was obvious that whatever those tubes were made of they were acting as a catalyst. It was almost like changing lead into gold, but much easier.

36

The day arrived to present herself before the licensing authority in Dublin. Nellie dressed herself up in her Sunday best for the occasion wearing her floral skirt which almost reached the floor. A smart off-white blouse with shamrock motifs embroidered on the collar and brown boots to finish the ensemble.

She had washed her hair and replaced the tight bun on the back of her head as she liked it. Even her glasses which were normally sticky with the residue of her product, were given a polish.

The bus had just pulled in to the kerb as she reached its stop. There were plenty of empty seats so she chose one which offered the best view for the journey into the city. It seemed to take all day to get there, in reality it was nearly three hours as it had to make many stops on the way.

The court-house was an impressive building. There were statues on either side of the entrance and fancy details around the windows on the first two floors. The top floor windows were much smaller and protruded from dormers in the roof.

As she went into the building Nellie noticed there were offices around the large reception area, each of these had a notice informing no one in particular what function they performed. There was an office for dog licences, another for fishing and game. In all there were about thirty of them. Most were apparently abandoned, as no one went into them or came out. Eventually she found what she was looking for. The customs office where she had to report before attending the licensing bench. She knocked on the door... ' Enter.' Nellie opened the door and went in after hearing the command following her tap on it.

"You are Mrs Eleanor Flanagan?" stated the pompous official sitting at his desk.

"I am sir, yes."

"Your address is Temperance Cottage, Gallon Lane, Kilmona. County Cork.?"

"That's right sir, yes." Jack Flanagan her long dead husband had named the cottage and the lane leading to it. He had a well developed sense of humour.

"And you are applying for a liquor manufacturer's licence. For this bench to grant that document it is necessary for your premises to be inspected for its suitability of purpose. This must be done within forty eight hours of this hearing by a senior Customs officer." Nellie was a little put out when she heard the conditions for gaining her piece of paper, she thought it was only going to be a matter of her attendance plus one hundred punts fee for it being granted.

It was a somewhat fidgety, thoughtful Nellie Flanagan sitting on the back seat of the bus carrying her back to the illicit distillery.

37

The phone call came to the farm five days after the discussion at the pub. Bill was as good as his word.

"I have arranged for you to meet my boss next Monday, I've given him a brief *resume* of the project and your requirement regarding funds. All you have to do is give him the info. as you explained it to me, I'm sure you'll get all the help you need to take the idea ahead"

"I can't tell you how much we appreciate this Bill. We must have dinner soon, the four of us. Rachel is looking forward to meeting Jane."

"That's OK Sean, my pleasure. Jane and I would love to join you both for dinner."

Bill's boss wasted no time in contacting the pair following his discussion with his junior colleague, the proposal appeared to be very sound the bank needed this kind of business.

The familiar sound of the telephone ringing brought Rachel running into the house from where she had been hanging out her basketful of washing. It was always the same, every time she left the confines of the cottage someone would ring. Still it could be important, not just another order for Mick's Mix.

"Hello is that Miss Flanagan?" the cultured voice asked.

"Yes." She answered not recognising the voice she heard.

"My name is John Shepherd I've been approached by Mr Fraser to see what we can do to help you with your request for funds. I think it would be best to talk about this at the bank. Is Mr O'Reilly there for a quick word ?"

"I'm afraid not at the moment Mr Shepherd, he's out on the farm somewhere. Can I get him to call you when he comes in ?"

"If you wouldn't mind, I would like a brief chat with him before we arrange the meeting at the bank." After finishing her chores Rachel went to find Sean, the sooner she did, the sooner they could find out what was happening. Sean wasted no time in dialling the number given to Rachel. It was quickly apparent that the upper echelons of the bank were getting a little 'tired' of their troublesome local manager. The confidential discussion which Sean and this Mr Shepherd had arranged was set up to find a way of 'moving' Jones to a smaller bank or shifting him sideways to Head Office so that they could control him.

The meeting at the bank was the following Monday at nine o'clock sharp, as soon as the bank opened. At this meeting would be Mr Shepherd, who happened to be a senior director of the bank, Bill Fraser, Sean and Rachel. Four against one. Sean thought this a little unfair on the hapless Jones and he was delighted. At last it looked as though their impasse with their stubborn adversary was going to be broken and their business would finally move on.

Monday arrived at the same time as an Atlantic depression. The rain seemed to say 'together we'll make his day!' Jones went to park his car in the reserved manager's bay, to find it occupied by a shiny black Jaguar saloon.

'Another good sign,' thought Sean who was watching from his very scruffy little Austin. He was amused to observe his nemesis scowling and talking to himself. When one of the young female cashiers ran through the rain clutching her umbrella Jones wound his window down shouting at her to get the idiot using his space to move it. *Now.* The unfortunate manager hadn't recognised the God-like figure of John Shepherd who had occupied the now lost, privileged space.

A red faced soon to be ex manager eventually parked his car at the only remaining space, which was furthest away from the bank's door There was no shelter from the deluge which now cascaded from the heavens and formed deep puddles to be negotiated by the miserable looking Jones. Rachel and Sean wouldn't have missed this if they had had to pay a fee.

When they were all in the manager's small office there weren't enough chairs for them all to sit down. Bill Fraser diplomatically suggested to the sodden junior official that he should obtain two extra chairs allowing them all a seat.

Jones went to press his intercom button in order to summon another employee to obtain these when John Shepherd quietly told him to fetch them himself, it would do no harm for Mr Jones to realise he was no longer in charge of the meeting.

"I've arranged this meeting so that you can have the chance to re-evaluate the proposals presented to you by Mr. O'Reilly. I've had a chance to briefly look over them and I agree with Mr Fraser who brought this to my attention that it could be a good deal for the bank. The manager who recognises this kind of opportunity and makes the decision to promote it by offering the necessary funding could enjoy a deserved promotion. Please do me the favour of explaining your objections to the scheme ?" The look of total surprise on Jones' face was observed by the rest of the group. Sean and Rachel understood exactly why the senior director had offered Jones the chance to save face and still think he had come out on top.

"Well Sir I've had a good deal of experience with farmers and that experience has taught me to be cautious when lending to them and this scheme requires large funding apparently. I wouldn't like to see this charming young couple suffer if it failed!"

"I see where you are coming from Derek. You don't mind if I call you Derek do you?"

"No sir, of course not."

"Well by my sums it looks like this couple cannot fail with this idea. If the bank grants them this loan the return they have already achieved will be more than treble the cost of the monthly repayments which means of course that the bank would benefit by the on-going profit which would be coming in for the foreseeable future. This could be many thousands of pounds.

Imagine how that would appear at Head Office!" The reality of the enormity of his own mistake was visibly dawning on the incompetent Derek Jones.

Humble pie by the bucket-load was called for, sullen silence was the reality.

38

The customs officer arrived at Temperance Cottage un-announced just as the potcheen was being decanted into the scaffolding tubes. Caught red-handed!

"You do I hope, realise that what you are doing is strictly against the law madam?"

"Against the law officer? we knew you were coming sometime so thought it a good idea to try and produce some hoo, er, potcheen ready for you to test. We had no idea that what we are doing is illegal did we Paddy?" she said in her very best cringing voice.

"That we didn't. God forbid we should break the law officer." Paddy added rising to the challenge of deceit. They were so good at their parts the officer felt distinctly sorry for the pair. They did indeed realise that the visit was imminent which was why all the copper pipes were polished to appear brand new as did the rest of the distilling equipment. Nellie stood looking over the top of her gold rimmed spectacles and her arms straight down her sides a true picture of innocence!

"Alright love I believe you although I doubt his Holiness would!

Pour me a small sample of the stuff I need to do some tests on it."

After half an hour using his testing equipment which consisted of all sorts of complicated tubes, bottles, thermometers and a particular scale for measuring the specific gravity, (whatever that is) he scribbled a lot of data into his official looking notebook. When he had finished he asked for a clean glass for a taste test. Having done the job for a number of years he was used to the effect of alcohol, even the raw stuff which came from the illicit stills.

However…. this was no ordinary potcheen. This had been taken out of one of the previous day's brews which had 'matured' in its scaffold tube, a nice casual ninety nine per cent proof sample! It was obvious the customs officer approved of this particular distilling, after the fourth glass he was entirely 'out of it'. The unsuspecting victim was carried into the cottage and laid out on the settee to sleep it off. The following day with a heavy hangover and after a 'hair of the dog' the official document was handed over. Nellie and Paddy were now going to be doing a legal job for the first time in both of their lives. A strange feeling!

39

The loan was quickly arranged with the reluctant Jones who made it clear to his clients that he wouldn't tolerate any late payments. It was going to be a difficult arrangement for the bank manager to live with, if he could punch above his weight at the start he could say 'I told you so' to his superiors if the project failed. Mind you he had to admit that the figures showed that it was extremely unlikely that failure was possible. He silently prayed that the impossible happened.

With this business now satisfactorily concluded Sean placed the order to supply the packaging plant urgently.

4⊘

"There is now no reason to delay organising our wedding." Sean stated in a matter-of -fact aside.

"No. I suppose not. When were you thinking of doing the business?" Rachel said in a similar tone, more in surprise at his nonchalant attitude than reacting in an excited way, after all this was what she had waited six years for.

The anti-climax of Sean's bland suggestion made her feel less than excited at having to organise her 'special day.' Sean noticed the dull response from his lovely partner with concern believing that she may have changed her mind about marrying him. He knew he would have to show a lot more enthusiasm about the event if she was to have the wonderful day she deserved. Tonight he would let her know that he wanted her to have the best of everything and they would organise the whole affair together, except for the surprises he was planning.

He had been at great pains to make sure that everything to do with this event would be beyond her wildest dreams. This wonderful person had transformed his life. It was now his turn to whisk her into another existence for the briefest of moments. By pretending to be off-hand about it all would maximise the treats he was storing up for her. Sean knew her so well now and he knew that she wouldn't be expecting anything out of the ordinary from him. It was going to be a treat for him to watch her excited reaction.

41

The new packaging plant arrived with a team of specialists to set the expansion in motion. It took three days to achieve the successful operation of the unit with thirty bags a minute now coming off the production line. Each one had the nutrient values printed on one side of the bright yellow five ply paper bags and on the other side, in bright red, was the company's logo Mick's Mix. Underneath this was the telephone number to contact so that even when empty they were advertising the product. Altogether a professional effect.

The first lorry load was despatched to a new large garden centre just outside Belfast and this would be followed every day into the future with huge financial success.

The bank loan for the plant was re-paid in full within three months of commencement of the operation much to the delight of the company's two young directors and the dismay of the ignorant Jones.

Rachel and Sean had spent many hours planning their wedding, all that was left to do now was to discuss the ceremony with the Father, arrange the date and select the venue for the reception.

With their rapidly swelling bank balance Sean knew he could really give his lovely girl the wedding of the century.

This was what it was all about and he wanted the whole neighbourhood to share the day with them, they would all be invited. When they had made a list of the people they wanted to attend the service they made a separate list for those they wanted to be at the reception afterwards. This last one was a very long one which included everyone they knew. There were a number of late additions which were dredged up from both of their memories of childhood.

This was going to be the biggest party the neighbourhood had witnessed.

Rachel made it her job to visit the stationers in Belfast as well as Enniskillen to choose the invitation cards, only the very best of everything was going to be used. They chose the venue and the wedding cake together. The hotel was going to be one of the big ones which sat on the edge of the Lough which had a fabulous view across the water. This was going to be where the photographs would be taken. Sean had a number of possibilities planned for their honeymoon destination, none of them would be local. Neither of them had ever flown before, short sea trips from school had been their only visits to 'The Mainland'.

Sean had secretly visited the travel agent to find out all he could about an island called 'Majorca' which he understood was somewhere in the Mediterranean not far from Spain. This place was very popular with the wealthy people so should be an ideal place to take his new bride for their honeymoon. The girl in the travel agent was extremely helpful in choosing the most expensive hotel on the island. Sean had asked her where she would like to stay if it had been her honeymoon they were planning. Naturally it had to be expensive…. Very.

The date of this jamboree was to be decided after a visit to the Church and discussion with the Father. They had known Father Robert as long as either of them could remember as regular Church-goers they were on fairly intimate terms with him.

The date was set. Saturday twenty seventh May at two o'clock. Saint Bernadette Church would welcome all the invited guests together with anyone wishing to accept the open invitation extended by the couple.

Father Robert was delighted with their decision to invite so many people to his church. At the last count there were one hundred and twenty two people officially invited plus the possibility of many more of the regular congregation who would be attending.

Father Robert surprised the couple by asking the Monsignor to conduct the service. When they were given this news Rachel was moved to tears as this was an honour. Her day was going to be exciting beyond her wildest dreams.

42

Nellie had taken full advantage of her elevation to legality by using some of the profit from Mickey Kelly's handling of the scaffolding company which was thriving due to the regular damage to buildings 'up north' by IRA bombs. It was getting difficult to provide enough tubes to erect the scaffolding required for some of the larger buildings. All-in-all a very satisfactory situation had occurred because of Nellie's earlier illegal activities!

The improvements to the distillery had included the building of an ultra modern factory with its accompanying storage and distribution units. There were seven people now working at the place. It had been necessary to take on the extra hands to cope with the demand for the finest 'Malted Miracle' produced in Ireland. Nellie herself was being bombarded with offers from rivals to take over her business.

These competitors jealously guarded their own recipes, some of which had histories going back many generations although none of them came anywhere near the potency of Nellie's brand which was now 'watered down' to five per cent alcohol level above the nearest opposition. The greatest challenge had been to produce enough of the 'tube-charged' variety. This was eventually overcome with the purchase of an old traction engine. Paddy realised that the boiler of this old machine would be an ideal hiding place for the newly brewed liquid. If the copper tubes in the boiler were removed and replaced with the scaffolding to complete the 'treatment'.

The quantity now being produced was exceeding demand by a substantial margin. The new method reduced the production costs by a considerable amount, distilling directly into the 'engine' cut out most of the intermediate handling so that they were able to sell the final brew to their commercial outlets at less than their competitors. Win -win! In very little time it was necessary to expand into larger premises.

After considering a nearby location Nellie and Paddy decided that the time was now right to move to Dublin. There were a few large premises which had been empty for many years on the dock-side there, one of these would be perfect. With expansion would come the need to export, where better than from here? New capital would be required. Nellie knew about Rachel and Sean's problem with their bank manager. These people couldn't be trusted. No bank would be given the chance to participate if she could help it!

"Is that you me darlin' girl?" Nellie said as she heard Rachel's voice through the receiver.

"Aye it is too Ma" was the reply when she recognised her mother's voice.

"It'll be Sean I'm wanting to talk to so it is."

"OK Ma but you and me could have a little chat for a while could we not?"

"That we could darlin'. How're ye keeping?"

"We're fine how's yerself then?" The conversation between them continued with trivial questions and answers for some time and the mood between them softened as it progressed. Rachel had never really forgiven her mother for getting Sean involved with the potcheen all those years earlier, now that she was involved legally there was room to put some of her anger aside and see if fences could be mended. The wedding plans were discussed at some length with Nellie who added ideas of her own. Rachel found it strange that she could allow her mother to become so involved with her plans without being resentful.

Now she was grateful and delighted to be sharing some of her happy thoughts.

Too soon it was time to pass the handset to Sean, who had been listening to the animated conversation between the two women he was most fond of, it was a strangely pleasant interlude for all concerned.

"Hi Nell. How's the booze industry going then?"

"It's great son, Paddy and me are thinking of moving up to Dublin soon, we've found a great place to put the new cooking pot, down at the dock-side in one of the old warehouses. You know the ones I mean?"

"I think so, sounds ideal to me Nell but you know your business. How can I help?"

"Well we'll need some extra cash to fit the place out and clean it up before we can start brewing, so I'm wonderin' if you want to be an official partner by buying into it? I've got the idea that you might have a few punts to spare now and I want to keep the business in the family. What d'ye reckon?"

"I'll have to discuss it with Rache' first of course, I like the idea. How much are you looking for?"

"About two thousand punts should give you a nice chunk of the firm and will see the job done."

"OK Nell I'll have a chat with Rachel and get back to you tomorrow."

43

The farm was now covering its costs entirely from the pig production although it must be said only just. No matter, it was no longer a source of constant worry. the by-product had saved the day! It was ironic that the effluent from these animals was providing the cash to purchase the food to produce the effluent. A sort of perpetual motion! An ideal situation had developed by pure accident. Regular payments from Nellie were making a valuable difference.

Sheila was now in complete control of the pig production unit which occupied the whole of the domestic non-flying area of the aerodrome.

Between the buildings was a collection of small grass paddocks which were unused by the animals as they were difficult to fence. It occurred to her that if they could obtain a small milling machine they could put the wasted areas to use by ploughing them and sowing barley this would supplement the feed and reduce further the production costs. Sean agreed and told Sheila to see if she could find a likely source of the necessary machinery and whilst she was at it, select a suitable building to house the plant.

There was even more to do on the farm now as the enthusiastic young manager was now keeping strict records of every action from servicing of the sows and gilts to weekly growth rates of the progeny.Altogether a totally professional approach. It was impracticable for Sean with his social commitments to deal with effectively. Sheila had become irreplaceable.

The ideal location for the milling project was the old RAF transport section which consisted of a line of garage style bays on one side of a large concrete square complemented by a line of tall closed buildings on the opposite side.

These buildings were used in the winter as temporary housing for the sows in the early stages of pregnancy. Sheila had found new homes for these animals so it would only need a few days work by the farm hands to clean them up and prepare them for their new use.

44

Sean and Rachel had spent the evening discussing the proposed investment in the 'Dublin Project' as Nellie's distillery was now called by the couple.

"I'm not sure about this Sean, look at the trouble her 'giggle juice' has caused I thought I'd lost you when you went to prison."

"I know love but I think now we can put all that behind us. It was a long time ago and it wasn't all her fault was it? I was as much to blame and you have forgiven me haven't you?"

"I suppose so but you stopped doing it when I asked you, she didn't did she?"

"I don't think she could, it's in her blood. I daresay if her blood was tested it would read at least fifty per cent alcohol!"

They both had a good laugh as they thought of the wiry little old lady 'doing her thing' with her pots, pitchers and pipes!

"Anyway what do you reckon? should we slip her the cash she needs?"

"If you want to, I suppose it can't do any harm if it's legal."

"It would be a great way for the pair of you to mend fences especially if you give her the money. She *is* your Mum after all."

45

The wedding day was drawing near, a nervous Sean who had lived with this beautiful person for nearly eleven years was fearful of 'taking the plunge' as though a piece of paper was going to change their relationship drastically. It was a strange sensation, he knew that many of their acquaintances frowned on people who lived as they did. If circumstances had allowed, they would probably have embraced the conventional way and lived apart until joined by the Church, most of those they knew understood this, those who didn't weren't worth worrying about.

Still, it preyed on Sean's mind as Rachel knew. She was glad they had spent the time together, it allowed them to get to know each other so well. What better basis for a sound marriage before children were on the scene?

May arrived with it's usual mix of warm sunshine one day raining and cold the next. With the arrival of spring came the annual visits to the farm of a variety of tradesmen. First of these was the representative of the animal foodstuff producer trying to gain an increase in his sales. As with most of these visitors he was directed to Sheila who took great pleasure in explaining her plans to be self sufficient with most of their requirements for the foreseeable future but would 'be in touch if we need anything'. The smile had vanished from his face as he left the yard less than half an hour after he arrived. Previous visits had lasted the best part of a morning, and a quarter of a bottle of whiskey! Now it was precious time wasted.

Another of these travellers was Paul Moffatt from the life insurance company. Sean was pleased to see him as he had a pleasant disposition and was really quite charming to Rachel having been completely taken in by her charm. It was not difficult to find oneself likewise in her company.

"Come in and sit down while I make us a cuppa" Rachel said.

"How're things in the insurance business these days then Paul?" enquired Sean of his visitor. "Very busy Mr O'Reilly, I can't stay too long as I've got five calls to do in the area today".

" I think we can scrap the formality don't you? just call me Sean"

"Thanks Sean, I would like to explain some new plans the company has developed and try to persuade you to take advantage of other ideas I have which should be to your advantage".

"Go on I'm listening."

"Well you will be pleased to know that your small investment is growing nicely." The agent proceeded to explain how the plan worked and on retirement the amount of profit was greatly in excess of the amount paid into it. Sean and Rachel were both impressed and agreed to consider increasing their contribution to the scheme, it also seemed a good way to invest some of their new wealth. After all they probably wouldn't want to work for ever. A pleasant hour passed before they concluded their business and Paul Moffatt left with a new contract signed in his briefcase.

"I will make sure that all these sorts of things are corrected to read Mr. S. and Mrs. R. O'Reilly next month."

"Everything financial will be in our joint names including the bank account." Sean added.

"Too true it will!" Rachel replied, meaning it.

A tap on the door attracted their attention. It was Sheila wanting to discuss her plans for the new milling plant and food mixer.

"I thought it was only a small mill you were after what's this mixer idea then?"

"It was only when I was talking to the salesman for the mill that I realised we would need the mixer to add the minerals and protein etcetera to make up the

rations. I might be asking you for the money for a pelleting machine soon too."

"You might get a rude answer!" Sean said in reply to her request.

"OK I'll look into it and see if we can afford to set the whole thing up for you Sheila. Make a list of everything you think is going to be necessary before I grab the begging bowl to offer our Mr Jones at the bank."

"Will we have to do that now Sean? Haven't we enough in the bank to buy these things?"

"Yes of course we have but I want to make the little sod squirm!"

"Really Sean, you're becoming paranoid over someone who isn't really very bright."

" I know, but I might as well try to make him work for his pay packet.

If I get the chance to rock his boat it would give me such pleasure! Anyway we might as well try and get a loan instead of drawing on our capital".

Rachel looked at him with a smile dancing on her face. She loved him. Even when he was cross!

46

Things were moving down in Dublin. Nellie had received the cheque from her daughter and was delighted that things didn't seem so strained between them anymore. It was important that the legal papers were drawn up as quickly as possible so that Rachel would know she appreciated this new spirit between them. The wharf building had cleaned up very well. Most of the expense incurred was for replacement of glass in all the windows and new exterior doors with the regulation locks needed to satisfy Customs. It was time to get the boilers fired up and start the distilling . Time wasted was money wasted.

There were only two weeks to go before the wedding. A new frock would have to be bought!

Life was more enjoyable these days. She was enjoying her new legal status and was becoming an accomplished business woman. It was no longer just a question of brewing a few gallons secretly and having to dodge the authorities. Even though this was probably why she had been so involved over the years. There was satisfaction to be gained from fooling the Garda!

The enormous increase in financial reward by being able to produce an ocean of the stuff and flogging it with the blessing of the authorities and the taxman had its advantages.

Helping her lovely daughter with her nuptials was so different from her previous experience she intended to enjoy the event to the full. At last she felt part of a family. No longer having to endure the loneliness which had been her life for so long.

47

Mickey Kelly was struggling with the scaffolding business as he had lost a large amount of his scaffolding poles. They were destroyed after being used on re-building blown up buildings by repeat visits of the IRA.

It had been difficult at times to manage without the use of the tubes which had been set aside. Even when the shortage was critical Paddy had insisted that these were *never* to be used As there was now no requirement for subterfuge by the Flanagan Empire Nellie decided to cut any further losses by giving the entire scaffolding business to Mickey who also decided not to risk any further losses by jacking the whole business in. He was disappointed that his first (and probably only) job as 'The Boss' hadn't lasted very long, however during his short spell as an executive he made a few useful contacts who would come in handy later in his life.

He felt a little aggrieved when Paddy was able to inform him of the reason for the prohibited use of those pipes. He would have loved to have been involved and reckoned he could have shifted twice as much of the stuff to his own group of misfit friends!.

48

Monday twenty second May nineteen sixty nine was a very busy day for Rachel. This was the beginning of her last week as a single girl, on Saturday she would become Mrs O'Reilly a new chapter was about to begin.

Before that could happen there was a great deal to organise which was going to be a lot of joy and fun. For so many years she had prayed for this week. At last it was here and she was going to relish visiting those posh shops to collect her wedding gown and the bridesmaids dresses. Sheila was given the day off to take the trip to Belfast with her, the florist was on her list of shops to visit. There was so much to organise, the button holes for the men in the party were easy they would be the traditional white carnations. After chatting with the florist the two women decided on lilies as the main blooms for the bride leaving the rest of the floral ensemble to be designed by the professional as this lady had obviously enjoyed many year's experience.

Next was the Bridal shop, in the window was an extravagant display of gowns adorning the mannequins some of which were made of pure silk with a price tag on them which caused the two to laugh out loud as they couldn't believe anyone could possibly afford to buy them. Rachel had already been for three fittings of the precious gown. It was necessary to make these trips into Belfast as she had lost a little weight since the date and venue were decided.

This was the last time the shop would be visited as she now had the expensive item safely in her hands. It was a different outfitters who were making the dresses for her two bridesmaids. This was their next stop. It was quickly apparent that they had made a good job when Sheila emerged from the changing room wearing her new dress. Looking at her now Rachel was worried that she was going to be out-shone by her attendants as Jane was going to look gorgeous also.

Sheila was thrilled when Rachel had asked her to be her chief bridesmaid. Bill Fraser's wife Jane was surprised and equally delighted to be also asked to take part in the important proceedings.

Sean and Rachel had enjoyed some special evenings with Bill and Jane and had become firm friends so it was natural that they should be included in their nuptials.

There was going to be a girls' night out on one of the last evenings of spinsterhood which would live in their memories, this too of course had to be arranged. It was not going to be a silly event as some of those who would be present at the party had enjoyed before their own 'special day'. All too often these had left the participants with Olympic hangovers which had somewhat spoiled the important event the following day. No, the evening would be an extravagant gourmet experience at the best restaurant in town. Why not the place Sean had taken her when he proposed? Rachel knew that Sean would want her to enjoy this part of the proceedings.

He had been busy in his own way. The official cars had to be booked the all important wedding ring was purchased and he had decided to buy a morning suit rather than rent one. He decided that owning this was an extravagance but it would come in handy for weddings or funerals he might have to attend in the future. After all ,he thought, they would only be more expensive next time he needed one. The logic was totally lost on Rachel even though she had just spent the larger part of one hundred and fifty pounds on her own outfit (which would never be used again!).

"I know we can afford it Sean but I do think it was a waste of money" Sean was getting a foretaste of what life being a married man was going to be like, he shrugged it off as he admired himself in the wardrobe mirror having tried it on… again.

"My word she's a lucky girl so she is" he said out loud to his reflection…..

49

The three attractive young women arrived at the restaurant and waited to be shown to their table. Rachel asked that the party should be seated away from the booths which had been the scene of her betrothal to her lovely man.

That was a private matter between the two of them. After the wine waiter had taken her order the party settled into a gossipy evening with plenty of joking and laughter until the subject of banks, managers and executives was casually brought into the conversation. Jane mentioned that Bill had received an important promotion, Rachel told her how delighted she was to hear this news.

"That's terrific Jane. Nobody deserves it more than he does."

"It was mainly because of the business you and Sean have done with the bank. Incidentally I know you didn't get on too well with Derek Jones did you?" Rachel's look at her friend confirmed the unspoken answer.

"I think you will be pleased with the new man who has taken over the branch from Jones."

"He's gone!"

"Oh yes, when John Shepherd found out how he had been treating clients he had him moved to Head Office to keep an eye on him. I gather he's hardly more than a filing clerk now. The bank won't sack him though, too difficult. He's a bit of a barrack room lawyer by all accounts."

"You've made my evening Jane. Sean will be over the moon when I tell him."

"I think you'll be too late love, aren't they together this evening?"

"The stag night. Of course. I hope Sean doesn't get too drunk celebrating, if he does I'll know who to blame!" The evening was a great success and the three went home in high spirits.

Among the dozens of guests at Sean's 'stag do' at the Foamin' Firkin pub were a few of his old pals from schooldays, Paddy McCormick and Bill Fraser.

All were enjoying the drinks and sandwiches. Sean had thought long and hard about who should be his Best Man. As he had been out of circulation for one reason or another for so long there was little choice for this important job.

His instinct was to choose Bill but he had known him for such a short time that it just didn't seem appropriate. The school chums were by now mere acquaintances. It had to be Paddy who had contributed so well to his present financial state and was a link to 'Aunty Nellie'. Paddy was less than enthusiastic about the idea as he had never done anything like it before! Sean convinced him that it was a good idea and helped him with his speech, much of which was based on mundane happenings since leaving prison. Paddy however had other ideas!.....

The bell for final orders was welcomed with shouting and swearing in what would appear to a foreigner to be unintelligible gibberish. It would have had a similar effect on anyone who came from the district who was sober!

The landlord ignored the protests and demanded that the assembly had; 'Five minutes before I throw you all out one by one.' It was quickly realised even in their inebriated state that this individual who was built like a brick outhouse would be perfectly capable of carrying out his threat! Twenty minutes later the last drunken body found it's way into the street preparing to find out which direction it needed to point to find its way home.

The whole week was disturbed by people making plans and arrangements for the coming event. Nothing was going to be left to chance, Rachel made sure of that.

After she was certain all was as organised as it could possibly be she rang the Father to see if Thursday afternoon would be suitable for the rehearsal of the service. Friday would be alright if it was not possible to fit them in during Thursday. In the event it had to be Friday as there was to be a funeral on Thursday.

Rachel managed to drag Sean and Sheila away from the pigs for the best part of the afternoon, they were all keen to go to this practice session as by now they were all feeling the reality of time for the event drawing near. One more night. Tomorrow morning would be hectic to say the least.

There were no misgivings by either of them just excited anticipation of what lay ahead. Sean wanted to make sure 'no other bugger was going to get a chance to steal his girl'!

Rachel had the picture in her mind of at least three children to mother within the shortest possible time. She went to sleep that night at the hotel which was hosting the reception. No way was she prepared to tempt providence by sleeping in the same house as her husband to be. She wasn't of course superstitious, it just wasn't done! The bed she lay in was supremely comfortable.

Dawn brought with it a cloudless sky, the sun's rays had woken her up as they poured through the window of her bedroom.

Rachel lay for a while enjoying the effect of shadows from the leaves of the horse chestnut tree which was displaying its creamy candles hiding a part of the sun which allowed the display on the wall opposite her bed. There was plenty of time before she would have to start preparing herself for this golden day. A leisurely breakfast in bed followed by a delicious soak in the enormous bath set her mood. Sheila joined her following her own breakfast to help with the business of preparation. First was the visit to the hairdressers to have that special treatment all brides must have before showing themselves off to their public. Today she would be a princess. Jane arrived just as they returned to the hotel, it was her job to check on the posies for all the important ladies together with checking the bride's bouquet and making sure there were no marks or other damage to the gown. This duty was carried out with utmost care. Everything was perfect, a bottle of the hotel's best champagne was brought up by a room service attendant, this was given as a courtesy by the hotel management and gratefully accepted by the recipients.

Sean awoke to the grandfather of all headaches. The clock on the bedside table was ticking in time to the throbbing in his head. The extra bender he'd been on after the practice for the ceremony was a mistake. What on earth was he doing allowing his best man to get him legless on the night before the wedding? What was the cure? A hair of the dog? Raw egg with Worcester sauce? The thought of any of these made him feel even more nauseous. Looking in the same mirror that told him he was handsome now revealed an ugly tramp with bloodshot eyes and a seven o'clock shadow which was exaggerated by the pallor of his skin. A large dose of liver salts followed by two cups of strong black coffee seemed to reduce the effect but only a little.

The ceremony was at two o'clock wasn't it? or was it two thirty? If I plan for two o'clock he reasoned there would be no chance of being late. After his shower and shave the mirror was telling yesterday's story again now. Altogether quite presentable. A little colour had returned to his face and the sickness he had felt was now only mild nausea. By the time he had made some breakfast, a boiled egg and piece of dry toast he began to feel better and was able to eat all he had prepared.

A tour of the farm woke him up fully and he really began to look forward once again to the day's happenings. Sheila had fed all the pigs and made sure that all the new arrivals were safe. The fattening houses would be cleaned out when the rest of the staff arrived. The time was still only eight thirty in the morning. Visiting the Mick's Mix plant showed that the whole empire was working efficiently. The order book was as usual, full. The sound of machinery humming away in the transport section was also gratifying. Feed was being mixed to keep the whole job printing money! Satisfied, Sean made his leisurely way back to the cottage to finalise his surprises for his new wife.

"Yes , if you wouldn't mind delivering it to the Manor House hotel just after two this afternoon. And please don't forget the message will you?"

"The lady is to be collected from the Manor House at a quarter to two precisely. You are sure you can do that?" The two most important tasks were now confirmed under control. All he had to do now was to freshen up in the shower and have another shave, he must look his best when he arrives at the Church. Paddy arrived at midday looking smarter that Sean had ever seen him.

The morning suit fitted perfectly even the tie was almost straight. His shoes however were on the scruffy side, the holes in the soles didn't matter too much as there was little possibility of rain this day. "Take em off and give em here." Sean ordered. Paddy did as he was told. Five minutes later Sean had got them shining as new, a coat of quick drying black gloss paint had transformed their appearance.

"Just leave them in the sun for a while they'll soon dry."

"OK Sean" Paddy answered knowing that he had let the side down somewhat. He had completely forgotten about needing black shoes to go with the suit. It was obvious really, green Wellington boots would look completely wrong! The shoes had been recovered from the back of the lorry where he had hastily discarded them over a month back, the inclement weather since then had done them no favours. By one o'clock the paint had completely dried, Success!

Sean was ready to go to fulfil the next part of his destiny by one thirty. He told Paddy to jump in the passenger side of the Austin but not to slam the door, the warning came a fraction too late.

Paddy was sitting in his seat alright however the door he had just roughly closed lay gently rocking on the ground beside the car! It was too late to try and repair the thing. They would have to go to the wedding as they were, only *very* slowly. The Austin was left in a lane near the church, the poor old jalopy had finally reached the end of its useful life. Actually that day had arrived at least three years previously but had been persuaded to work into its retirement.

Sean and his best man walked away from the wreckage towards the gate leading into the churchyard, it was five minutes to two as the pair entered the church and proceeded to their reserved places; Paddy to his seat next to the already seated Bill Fraser on the front of the pews, Sean sat at the end of the row next to the aisle to await the arrival of the bride.

As the large hand on his wristwatch reached two o'clock the babble of conversation from the congregation had dropped to an occasional whisper as the filled church waited in anticipation of the arrival of the star turn.

The red second hand had to revolve a further five times before the organist broke into the familiar opening bars of the wedding march. As one the gathering turned to stare as the beautiful girl stepped into the aisle on the arm of Mickey Kelly who had been delegated the task of giving her away.

There was an audible collective gasp. Sean could hardly believe the sight of Rachel dressed as she was in her figure hugging white gown its silver embroidered bodice caught the occasional bright light making her look like a beautiful doll. The congregation was now on its feet smiling at her. Rachel returned their warm greeting with a dazzling smile of her own. The net veil she wore couldn't hide the smile or the pretty face which radiated her happiness.

The two bridesmaids complemented her by being just attractive enough to show her off. They were dressed in their oyster coloured dresses, carrying their posies of red roses which contrasted to advantage. The whole effect seemed perfect. Sean moved into the aisle to be beside her as Sheila took Rachel's bouquet from her. They moved together to the seats which had been placed to face the body of the church so that everyone present could observe the proceedings and the faces of the couple when they took their vows. After they had taken their seats and the priest introduced the Monsignor, the service commenced. He began with the traditional rite of the Nuptials asking them in turn:

"Do you come of your own free will to give yourselves to each other in marriage?" He then asked them if they would honour and love one another as husband and wife for the rest of their lives and would they accept children from God lovingly, and bring them up according to the law of Christ and his Church?

They were able to answer sincerely that they would. The Solemn Promise followed where they joined hands and declared their consent before God and the Church. The Monsignor then asked Rachel 'Do you take Sean O'Reilly here present for your lawful wedded husband to have and to hold from this day forward, for better or worse, for richer or poorer, in sickness and in health. To love and cherish until death do you part?" Rachel turned towards Sean with tears glistening in her eyes as she quietly responded;

"Yes, I do".

The ritual continued with Sean's vows and as he placed the gold band on her finger he too had tears in his eyes.

"May the Lord in His goodness strengthen your consent and fill you both with His blessings. What God has joined together let no man put asunder."

After these last words from the priest were said Rachel and Sean holding hands saw that handkerchiefs were fluttering around their friend's faces.

They seemed to float down the aisle as the choir accompanied by the organ proclaimed the culmination of the service with a beautiful rendering of Rachel's favourite hymn, Panis Angelicus.

Photographs of the wedding group outside the church took nearly half an hour. The couple radiated their happiness which was infectious and the photographs would bear testimony to it.

When the time came to leave the church for the reception the first of Sean's surprises arrived at the gates. A landau carriage pulled by two immaculate grey horses. Sean offered his hand to assist his bride as she climbed into the carriage, when she was seated he followed her into this unusual but exciting form of transport. As he expected she was genuinely delighted with his thoughtful surprise.

The hotel was some distance from the church and so they were able to enjoy in comfort the beauty of the countryside at a leisurely pace. The warm spring sunshine completed the enjoyment of the ride, there was no need for words. The rhythmic stutter of the horses hooves on the roadway was all the sound needed to fill their minds with the memory of this wonderful day. After what seemed like a few moments the driver commanded his charges to stop, which they accomplished gently. A liveried footman stepped to the side of the carriage and opened the small door to allow the occupants to alight. Mr. and Mrs. O'Reilly walked slowly into the foyer of the hotel hand in hand gazing into each other's eyes. The casual observer would think they had only just fallen for each other.

The hotel's manager met them as they entered, behind him a waiter hovered waiting to give them their first glass of champagne. This could only be handed to them after they had greeted their guests. First to arrive by taxi was the bridesmaid's group which included Paddy, Bill and Nellie. They took their places in a line to welcome the large retinue of guests. The reception itself continued to be a joyful occasion. Speeches were made, Sean's was for him a formal one he welcomed the guests in a charming way including some mild topical stories including how he met Bill and Jane and directing some warm remarks to his new mother-in-law, he ended with his admiration of Rachel's loyalty during his incarceration and his pride in now being her husband.

Paddy rose to his feet to deliver the toast to the bridesmaids which was done in a serious manner before attempting a jocular vocal annihilation of his friend the groom! The happy and successful event went on well into the evening with Rachel looking gorgeous but a little tired when the time came for the couple to leave. This they did soon after ten o'clock.

Rachel knew that they were going to spend their honeymoon 'somewhere abroad' as Sean had been insistent on her obtaining a passport. This evening though they were going to spend at this hotel beside the beautiful Lough.

Paddy had been given the keys to the brand new Aston Martin sports car which Sean had secretly purchased with his new found wealth. He chose a silver coloured one which would be appropriate for the occasion. Paddy had done a good job on it with the gold ribbon tied through the windows making it look like a big birthday gift. This was Sean's other surprise for the day.

They awoke very early that Sunday morning as an early start was needed to drive themselves to the airport. Paddy and Nellie were waiting for them in the car park to wish them 'Bon

Voyage' and to retrieve the car keys. It was Paddy's final task as Sean's best man to return the new car to the farm for safe keeping until they returned from their long awaited holiday.

The flight to Majorca was a pleasant experience for them both, Rachel had the seat by the window so that she could enjoy the view. The attractive young stewardess offered them refreshing drinks and even served them with a hot meal which was another novelty.

As the aircraft descended Rachel felt her ears 'pop' as the air pressure changed. Everything on the ground seemed to grow larger until there was a slight bump when the wheels touched down on the smooth runway.

On leaving the aircraft everything was so bright. The strong Mediterranean sunshine lit the scene with an intensity that Rachel had never known at home in Ireland. This was going to be a lovely, different time to enjoy each other's company.

The newly-weds spent their days swimming in the sea or sunbathing. It was so good to feel warm even in the water. The strength of the sun soon made their bodies change colour, after the initial sting of sunburn they soon developed a tan which made them almost appear as strangers to each other. Everything was perfect, the memory of their recent wedding the extravagant new car and this enchanting honeymoon was so completely different to anything that went before.

It was a very happy relaxed couple who arrived home two weeks later.

50

After their marriage Rachel was determined to start her family as soon as possible and so it was a delighted Sean who was casually informed one morning that he was going to be a father in eight months time!

The pig farm was almost completely out of his hands now. Sheila had been a success from the day she arrived on the premises and so it gave Sean and Rachel pleasure to promote her to be official manager of the pig business being an extra 'thank-you' for her short stint as the perfect bridesmaid at their wedding.

Mickey was now in total charge of the fertiliser plant which was now famous country wide although there was now not enough 'product' coming from their own pigs and so Mickey had acquired further supplies from three other farms in the area.

These extra supplies allowed him to produce speciality products for different plant requirements. The fragrant smell of fowl droppings and the more frequent delivery of liquid cattle effluent left a permanent pungent whiff wherever one was on the property itself or anywhere within two miles on the down-wind side of the unit! One best selling product was the manure which was purchased from the local racehorse stables was diverted straight to the new mushroom farm which had an insatiable demand for it.

Mickey was surprised and again delighted to be entrusted with the responsibility of management and rose to the challenge successfully. He was constantly looking for opportunities to expand business.

The O'Reilly businesses were now producing large profits which Sean was channelling into a pension fund which would eventually sustain all the employees when they were too old to work anymore. A worthwhile and satisfying goal.

5 I

As Rachel's pregnancy developed she showed worrying signs of distress, she found trouble getting enough sleep and suffered from nausea constantly, it was obvious to them both that things were not progressing smoothly although the doctor had said he didn't think there was anything to worry about. After four months of this discomfort and many visits by the district nurse, Sean went to see the doctor to insist on a second opinion for his wife. She was taken into hospital the following day and was attended by the gynaecological consultant who examined her and told the attending nurse to arrange for her to be placed in one of the private side wards for constant observation. Rachel protested as she was sure there couldn't be anything seriously wrong,.....could there?

Sean was naturally extremely worried that something might happen to threaten his beloved wife and their un-born infant.

"You *must* stay here and do as you are told" Sean insisted.

"But darling I don't want to be here. I want to come home with you."

"The doctors and nurses say that it is very important that they monitor your blood levels for the next few days at least. Please don't make a fuss. Just for once do as you're told!"

Rachel reluctantly accepted the need for her to stay in the hospital. In fact she had to stay in the hospital for the rest of her pregnancy. Toxaemia was the diagnosis of her condition and it was deemed vital that the mother-to-be should have total bed-rest if there was going to be any chance of saving the child. The couple were upset when they were given this unpleasant news. They assumed everything would be fine, surely nothing could possibly hurt their baby could it? Sean visited her every day trying to cheer her up and break the interminable boredom of these long days and longer nights. Books on caring for new baby, recipes for energy giving food for new mothers. Even books for the new father were read from cover to cover, nothing helped. Sean would find her crying when he peeped round the door to her private room on his arrival sometimes. If only there was some relief from the anxiety she would feel better.

This couldn't happen, every day she became more morose and distant.

Every week she grew a little fatter her temper wasn't helping the situation either. She would explode at the slightest irritation. Calling Sean names and blaming him for her condition. Sean loved her too much to respond in his own defence, he knew it was the illness which made her say such hurtful things to the one person in the world she trusted and adored. It was all so frustrating.

To make matters worse it was now August and it had been the hottest summer in living memory with the windows of her room wide open it was still stiflingly hot and she was constantly soaked with perspiration. When will this end!

Mercifully on the night of August the tenth her waters broke. At one thirty the following morning little Maria was born.

'There is room for a little cautious optimism' was the comment from the doctor who telephoned Sean to announce the birth.

"What do you mean by that?" queried the new father.

"We had to use forceps to assist the delivery." He replied. The sick child was removed from her mother immediately after birth and placed in an incubator. Rachel had the fleetest of glances at her daughter before she was taken away from her. Sean however was able to observe his daughter through the Perspex cover of the incubator which was in the nursery and insisted on seeing her as soon as he arrived at the hospital each day. He loved gazing at her with her dark hair just like her mother's which she seemed to have plenty of, and those eyes! when she briefly opened them were deep blue like her daddy. This was going to be a beautiful woman one day no doubt about it, he was so proud. Rachel had been too ill to stand after the birth and so had to stay in bed to gain strength before she could join her husband by the incubator to look at their new offspring.

Three days after the birth Rachel began to look her lovely self again and was preparing to take her first peep at the little devil who had caused so much trouble.

"I think you'd better sit on the bed dear." The nurse said as she came into the room.

"Is your husband here yet?" she enquired.

"No but he won't be long, can I go and see her now?" Rachel implored. "Just a moment I think the doctor wants a word with you both first."

The tone was ominous, Rachel sensed that there was something wrong.

Suddenly she was frightened. Sean had just arrived when the consultant entered the little room some minutes later.

"I am so sorry. As you are aware I had to use forceps to help with the birth and the cord was wrapped around her neck causing trauma to her brain. I'm afraid the next few hours are critical!" They couldn't believe what they had just been told. All those months in bed being cared for to make sure no harm would come to either mother or child. It was time to pray,

Sean went to see their priest that day together they prayed for a miracle.

Sean arrived at the hospital just as his little daughter died…..

They had to put their lives back together after losing their baby. Both of them threw themselves into helping the local community, they knew that in time the hurting would lessen but they would never ever forget.

52

As the businesses were all very productive and financially very successful. The couple were now eager to put some of their energy back into the community which had supported them over these last dozen years. The village needed a community centre, many attempts had been made in the past to raise the necessary funds to build a suitable venue for the variety of purposes the villagers needed. The older members wanted a meeting place, somewhere comfortable to hold whist drives. The Women's Institute, Mother's Union and various other organisations also needed a room to congregate. It had always been difficult to encourage new membership when the meetings were in individuals homes. The younger members of the community were living with relatives who would object to being invaded by gossipy women! The youth needed somewhere permanent to hold disco dances and play their indoor sports.

In effect a multi-purpose hall was needed to encourage the young people to stay in the area and build the community into a thriving society. Sean and Rachel were determined to raise the necessary finance to make the dream a reality which was to become their new passion. The starting point for their project was their own bank account. Sean wrote a cheque for one thousand pounds to as he put it, 'buy the first brick.' The villagers joined in enthusiastically, any and every money raising idea was examined at the weekly gathering in the Church hall. Ideas ranged from weekly whist drives to the raffle of a new car.

Some wag suggested that Sean's old Austin be resurrected, repaired and used as the first prize!

It took nearly two years to raise the required cash, it was Rachel who signed her personal cheque for the final five hundred pounds needed to reach the necessary target.

A party was organised in the village hall to celebrate their collective success. People came and went throughout the evening some for only a few minutes just to make sure their support was noticed.

A community spirit was developing which in turn was bound to attract new residents to move into the village. Numbers had declined over the past decade. The world war had claimed so many and others had moved away as a result.

Building new dwellings would inevitably follow which would benefit everyone. The atmosphere was so positive that everyone became impatient to be involved in the money raising activity which was feverishly encouraged by Rachel, who took it upon herself to be the 'ideas secretary' for the villagers.

53

The little cottage which had been their home for the last ten years now seemed inadequate as it was necessary to entertain business contacts and friends on a fairly regular basis, the space in the cottage was insufficient for this purpose and so Sean suggested to Rachel that they should apply for planning permission to build a much larger family residence. A local building firm was asked to do the building work after consultation with Rachel on its layout. This part of the planning Sean knew was essential. Kitchens, bedrooms bathrooms were her domain, designing these would be her interest. Obtaining a mortgage to pay for it all was Sean's. He had developed a useful business relationship with the new manager at the bank Simon Forbes, it was to him that Sean went for advice and the information he needed to progress with his plans.

Simon explained that the bank didn't provide mortgage facilities but there were companies who specialised in them. Sean asked Simon to make some enquiries on his behalf.

It was obviously going to take time to organise the building of their new home and it would keep the pair of them on their toes as they were required by the village fund raisers to be available to solve everyone else's problems as well!

Having by now had a good deal of experience with problem sorting in their own lives, the villagers naturally depended on them and they were happy to be able to oblige. Trivial local problems kept their minds off the sad loss of baby Maria. For this they were both grateful.

54

Nellie was now entering her eightieth year. She was chair person of the Kilmona Whiskey Corporation and so she was responsible for the overall product policy together with the employment of a large workforce. The combination of these factors meant a stress level that people half her age would have had difficulty coping with. She was beginning to feel this stress and was showing it. Forgetting important meetings with clients and officials. Regular headaches were a part of her everyday life which were sometimes so bad she had to tell Paddy to take over her appointments He was capable of any task she asked of him, often better than herself.

It came as little surprise one day when she suggested that he take over as chairman permanently which he was expecting some day anyway. When she asked him, he accepted on condition that she would remain on the board of directors as an adviser. Paddy rang Sean to tell him the news.

As a director of the company he had to be informed and be asked for his blessing. Paddy was aware that Sean had a financial interest in the firm and probably had a claim to take over himself. In the event Sean was able to assure his old chum that he was sure Nell had made the correct decision, after all he had had so little to do with the distillery since it became a legal business. This was the best and obvious way forward.

"If there is anything I can do to help Paddy, get in touch. And Paddy, look after Nell won't you?"

"That goes without saying Sean I love her like she was me Mum. She's me best friend next to yourself of course".

Sean was relieved when the changes had been made, he knew that Nellie had been unwell for some time and was going to suggest to her that she should hand over the reins soon. This had saved him an uncomfortable confrontation with the old lady, it would also set Rachel's mind at rest she had been worrying too. A new chapter was beginning.......

55

Now in the nineteen seventies, there was a massive growth in consumerism led by the United States of America followed by the UK and most of the developed countries of Europe. There were many opportunities for enthusiastic entrepreneurs to make vast fortunes which in turn encouraged bankers and city dealers to make their pile.

Some of these were efficient, clever people others were greedy manipulators even more were just plain crooks, it was impossible to identify the honest amongst them. People like the O'Reillys were dependent on this group to invest the profits from their legitimate business interests in order to obtain a reasonably good 'rate of return' for their hard earned cash. A vast range of 'products' were offered, some were risk free government issue gilt edge shares which paid a low rate of interest but were completely safe. There were Post Office products which offered even less. Anyone with large sums to invest would look to the city via stock brokers or their accountant for advice. Sean and Rachel were now in the market to find a suitable vehicle for investment.

Bill Fraser was asked for his advice as was Bill's old boss John Shepherd.

"We want to invest safely Bill, obviously we want the best return we can get but not with a lot of risk. It has taken so long to get to where we are we want to be able to give our family a good start in life."

"Presumably when you have increased it….. the family that is!" Bill suggested.

"Of course!" laughed Rachel.

"Why don't you have a word with John Shepherd, he's had a lot of experience with the bank's wealthier clients and has contacts in the city?"

"That sounds a good idea Bill he seems on top of this money business. I'm afraid I haven't a clue about investments" replied Sean.

"Well I can't agree with you completely on that Sean. Looking at your present business success I reckon you are well versed in the 'money business'. Pigs, potcheen and plant food don't seem to be too much of a failure."

Bill contacted John Shepherd who promised Sean he'd give him a few names of people to contact who could advise him. Who to trust and which investment companies had performed well over the previous few years. Rachel agreed that it was time to start thinking seriously about saving money rather than always spending it! She was desperately keen to try for another baby, the pain of her loss was still there but it wasn't so sharp now. A new baby would be a wonderful way to move on. Sean, she knew, felt the same.

Their love-making would be pursued with enthusiasm and hope. This effort was rewarded a few weeks later when Rachel was able to announce one evening that she was 'on the way' again! Sean was cautiously delighted he was also aware now that things could go disastrously wrong when making babies. He asked Rachel to be careful and not to get too excited until the new member of the family was safely born and thriving. They decided not to tell anyone until it was obvious she was pregnant by the size of her belly.

Sean had a long interesting meeting with John Shepherd, after discussing the idea of investing some money John advised Sean to make sure that his portfolio would be a mixture of different types of investment. Some of it should be in commercial property maybe some in 'blue chip' shares and possibly some in a hedge fund, whatever he decided it should be with a reputable company.

"I've heard that the British Government is going to sell off the airfield Sean. If I were you I'd be inclined to see if you could make a bid for it. I believe it is the whole aerodrome they want to sell. About three hundred acres, if you could get the whole site think what you could do with that!"

"What about the price though do you have an idea what sort of figure they will be looking for?"

"From what I've been able to find out they're wanting a quick deal. With the security problems here with the paramilitaries they would readily accept a fairly low sensible offer."

"Agricultural land is about one hundred pounds an acre now" said Sean.

"Do you think they would take fifty?"

"Why not try and see?" said John.

"They can only say 'no' can't they?" He made the offer in writing to the Crown agent in Belfast the same afternoon, if he was successful he'd have to find the funds quickly.

Rachel was being very careful with this pregnancy, there was going to be no heavy physical exertion but she was making sure that her daily exercise programme was carefully planned. Walking to the village which was about a mile from the farm began every day's routine. She wouldn't carry any heavy shopping. It would normally only be a newspaper or the occasional women's magazine. Sean was a concerned father-to-be and clucked like an old hen whenever he thought she was doing too much. Regular visits to the doctor for 'check ups' meant that every chance of a healthy infant was indicated. Nevertheless it was a worrying nine months for them both.

The possibility of them buying the aerodrome was a temporary financial headache, now that they were intent on building their new house it meant that they would have to have a mortgage to finance it. The advice they had received from their broker said property was the safest and most profitable way to invest their savings. Having done this it meant that practically all of it was now tied up in long term investment portfolios which were difficult to reclaim without substantial penalty, as a result any finance required would have to be borrowed Sean didn't like the idea at all. All his life he had always saved for any extravagant purchases, living in this new era he found difficult. Simon Forbes explained in great detail that the modern way to live was to borrow from banks or building societies it was perfectly normal to use other people's money when financing expensive capital projects like they were planning it was just 'business'.

"Look Sean, if people didn't borrow from the financial world there wouldn't be any need for banks would there? Besides, the profit from any loans we give are used to pay the shareholders and we mustn't forget the annual bonus the boss needs to keep his missus in fur coats now must we?" It all made perfect sense when put like that. Business was just that…. Business.

The reply from the Crown agent's office arrived by return of post. Struth! they must be keen to get rid of it thought Sean when he recognised the logo on the reverse of the envelope.

'Dear Sir' it read 'I have the pleasure to inform you that Her Majesty's agent has accepted your tender for the property known as… etc. etc.'

"Wow, that's great." Sean exclaimed as he read the letter aloud to Rachel.

"It means we will be totally self sufficient in barley and wheat with what we can grow on all that extra land."

"But what about all that wasted land where the roads are?" Rachel responded. " Roads?-what roads?"

"All those great big straight ones that run all over the fields"

"Oh you mean the runways, they could be useful in the future. Anyway the price we have agreed is way below the normal land price around here."

"Won't we need new tractors and all the other stuff if we're going to be running a farm?"

"Not straight away no. We can get most of the work done by contractor, try and think positively. Better still let *me* do the worrying please, you just get on making that perfect baby!"

Simon was very supportive at the bank and Sean couldn't help comparing him to his predecessor. There was no way they would come this far in so short a time without the pragmatism of his new acquaintance at the bank.

Bill was becoming more and more interested in the progress of his young friends, in fact he was a little envious of them as he told them at one of their regular meetings.

"*You* are envious of *us*!" stated a surprised Sean after it was said.

"Indeed yes, Jane and I would love your sort of lifestyle, not being cooped up in an office most of the time would be wonderful!"

"There's a lot to be said for the financial security of your job Bill not to mention the long holidays and bonus cheques."

"You have a point of course Rachel. Seriously though, now you can measure your own financial progress with the sky being the limit if you carry on developing new businesses at the rate you have been doing." Sean was a little surprised at the frankness of his friend. Money matters were usually taboo when they were socialising.

"If you're not careful I'll be asking you to 'join the board' soon!"

"I think you'd be surprised at my response to that if it was seriously offered" came the response. Sean was visibly shaken by the remark. A senior banker interested in joining them, what a brilliant idea!

"Well I'm sure we can trust him but I'm certain we couldn't afford to pay him the sort of salary he must be getting from the bank." Rachel said, Sean had to agree. The idea was shelved for the time being.

There were important decisions to be made regarding the proposed building plans. First was a visit to the Building Society to see about that mortgage….

The couple's plan to build was entirely dependant on getting this loan. The estimate from the builder for all the works necessary to achieve this was a seemingly huge amount, inflation in the building industry wasn't helping. With the nineteen seventies came almost daily increases in the price of materials. It seemed just about everyone wanted to buy their own property now. A seller's market was developing.

"I am allowed to offer you a ninety per cent loan Mr O'Reilly. Can you give me evidence of your income for the past three years?" The manager was very polite with his questions, Sean felt a little uneasy having to answer some of them.

"Forgive the question but why do you need those figures?" he asked.

"It is the British government's policy to restrict the size of loans to the ability to repay the monthly instalments. This can only be ascertained given the actual income of the prospective client." This seemed a pretty fair way of doing things Sean thought. With the swelling demand there had to be a sensible way of ensuring the loan companies would not be lending to people who obviously couldn't afford the repayments forcing the lender to recover his money by repossessing and reselling the property. There would be a domino effect in the financial markets if unlimited lending got out of hand.

"Moreover it is a further requirement that a percentage of the loan is repaid alongside the interest we charge on that loan. On your side of this arrangement we, the Society, have to give you a fixed rate of interest over the duration of this loan which can be either over twenty five years for someone under thirty years of age or as in your case over a period of twenty years. I hope that's clear to you Mr O'Reilly?"

"What about my wife's income surely that can be included can't it?"

"I'm afraid not sir, no. The calculation can only be done on the main bread-winner's income."

The sums were done and it was just within the budget when the agreement was signed. Rachel would understand that things were going to be a little tight for a while, still the house building process could begin straight away.

Planning permission arrived for their new home, the sooner the building began the better. The architect thought it a little odd that more attention was being shown to the nursery design than the kitchen which was most unusual.

In fact it was definitely unusual, the woman of the house was *always* more interested in the kitchen than any other room.

It was a touch of *déjà vu* when the truck arrived carrying the scaffolding for the new house, it was impossible not to think of the of the hooch business!

Rachel was nearing full term with her pregnancy; all the indications were good, this time there was no sign of any problem. She was radiating good health apart from some mild nausea early on she was enjoying her condition.

When the time approached for the arrival she woke Sean at two in the morning to tell him it was time to go to the maternity home.

"Have you got everything you need? What about a clean nightie? undies? Hurry up and get ready."

"Don't panic! There's plenty of time Sean." It wasn't like him to be like this but after the last time he felt nervous about the whole business and wouldn't calm down until she was safely in the confines of the maternity home. It was only twenty minutes from the moment Rachel woke him up until she was in the car and they were on their way. The nursing home was only about ten minutes careful drive away.

When he was satisfied that she was comfortable he left her to the nursing staff to do any worrying that needed doing, one of them assured him that was not his concern. He felt a little reassured when they told him that they had the whole business well under control, however there was no sleeping for the rest of that night for him!

The kettle had been refilled and boiled at least half a dozen times before the first light of dawn crept into the kitchen. When the phone rang at six minutes past seven in the morning he had the receiver off its cradle before the first ring had faded.

"Hello? Yes. A Boy! Born at two minutes past seven, seven pounds four ounces Mother and child both doing very well! Thanks, thank you so much."

Sean almost threw the handset back on its resting place in his joy and excitement. The Aston Martin's wheels hardly touched the ground as it raced at full throttle down the road leading to the maternity home, Rachel was ready for him. When he arrived she was sitting up in bed smiling broadly and cradling what looked like a very small doll in her arms. Sean crept over to the bed as if making any sound at all or sign of hurry might damage the precious bundle!

Pulling the shawl aside which was hiding part of his new son's face he stared in wonder at the perfect features of the sleeping baby. His tiny fingers had delicate little nails already. As he kissed Rachel a feeling of extreme tenderness overwhelmed the little group. Sean had never in his life experienced anything like the feeling he now had. He had adored Rachel from the time they were children at school together.

Looking at her now with the infant at her breast he simply worshipped her. Rachel couldn't take her eyes off the tiny person, her son who was attached to her in this way she loved this feeling. After what seemed like five minutes but which turned out to be over two hours a nurse came into the room and suggested to Sean that he allow his wife a little time to get some sleep as 'she has been rather busy!' He took the not too gentle hint and left her to have her well earned rest.

Suddenly he felt tired, tired but very happy maybe he should get some sleep before he told the whole world that his son had now arrived and would soon be a huge part of everyone's life. Everyone the couple knew anyway. Sean made it his priority to give the happy news to Nellie all the relevant details of time, weight hair colour etcetera. He knew that all personnel in the distillery would be given all these details in the shortest possible time, Nell wasn't normally a sentimental person however this was her first grandchild.

Her grandson was the exception and she almost burst with pride as she passed on the details as though she had been personally responsible for the new arrival!

Rachel was soon back on her feet and back at the farm, her time was now taken up with a lively little boy who was always hungry.

56

The building society accountants had calculated the income figure for granting their mortgage. The figure was based on Sean's three years salary which was now sufficient to cover the basic building costs of the new house.

They would have their new home before the new arrival started to walk, right now he needed a name. They had decided to wait until the baby had arrived safely before names were chosen. They were not going to tempt fate.

Suggestions were tossed to each other and rejected. Why was it so difficult to choose a name? Eventually there was a short list of five from which to decide.

Rachel said she wanted a traditional Irish name. Sean was more open minded so long as it was not going to embarrass the lad at school he didn't really mind. Rachel selected Liam. After considering every Irish boy's name, Sean eventually chose William as his son's second, after their good friend Bill Fraser.

A series of calls to finance companies were made to select investment programmes for Liam's future financial security. Paul Moffatt from the Farmers Union insurance was particularly helpful in setting up a monthly payment plan to start saving for the boy's future.

57

The Crown agent arrived for their arranged meeting five minutes early. Sean was feeling nervous as this deal was by far the biggest thing he had ever been involved with. It wasn't that he didn't think he was up to dealing with a Crown agent it was more that he hadn't yet decided how he was going to develop the extra land to justify its purchase. The meeting turned out to be a formality. The document was passed over by the agent which had to be signed by both parties and in return for this piece of paper a cheque for fifteen thousand pounds was signed and passed to the government official. On reflection, Sean realised that it was this signing of the cheque with such big numbers which was the cause of his uneasiness, he had never seen such a valuable piece of paper in his entire life and it was scary!

Young Liam William was making his presence felt in the household by the frequent use of his lungs. And what an appetite!

It was now Rachel's habit each morning when the weather would allow, to take O'Reilly junior for a walk in his pram, usually to the village but sometimes when the sun shone the route would change to go past the old control tower (which had been the limit of their farm) and over the airfield to the village, until now the area had been someone else's responsibility.

What *had* they taken on? The airfield seemed huge and it took a good half an hour around the old taxiway to reach the exit gate on the far side. The giant runways seemed to go on forever, these things were at least three times the width of the main road into Belfast! What a waste of good land Rachel thought.

Sean had felt much the same when he first examined their latest acquisition but it didn't take him long though to realise there could well come a time when a practical use for some of these Tarmac behemoths could be put to good use.

His thoughts were shared by Bill who suggested a new use every time he and Sean spoke. For now all that mattered was to cultivate the land intersected by them. Barley and wheat, the basic ingredients for the pig rations would be sown here, Sheila had already worked out how many acres of each would be needed to balance the rations. Between them Sheila and Sean had investigated the most likely local contractors, to plough up all the grassland in preparation for spring sowing of the vital seed. This research produced tenders from most of their farming neighbours whom they knew from village social events. They were on friendly terms with them all. Sean decided that the fairest way of allocating the work amongst them would be to have a meeting with all the applicants together to allocate each share. No one it seemed was making much of a living from their own farms and the possibility of earning extra by helping Sean and Rachel was appealing. Rachel suggested that a barbecue on the Saturday following this meeting would encourage the wives, families and all the young un-married couples to attend the gathering which might lead to a sort of local agricultural co-operative. Sheila was very enthusiastic as this might benefit her own family in the future. The meeting was arranged for a weekend and as it was summer the hope was that the weather would be kind. If not, the control tower would double as a café.

Most of the farmers arrived late. There was always an excuse for farmers to be late, even for important meetings with officials and so it was no surprise to Sean that this meeting was almost an hour delayed in getting started.

He opened the meeting by giving the gathering a warm welcome and a brief summary of his plans for the pig farm and the need for producing the extra cereals. He went on to inform them that there was a wide variation of rates per acre demanded by them.

"If you would look at these figures you can see for yourselves what I mean. I haven't put any names to the numbers so no one need be embarrassed, obviously I want to pay you as little as possible and all of you naturally want to be paid as much as you can get." The gathering chuckled thinking that Sean was joking.

"I would like to suggest that you spend the next hour or so having a look at the figures and have a chat amongst yourselves, a sensible compromise is needed. Maybe Arthur Kinsella as the owner of the largest farm amongst you could act as a sort of chairman…? Thank you Arthur.

There was some heated discussion as one or two of the men who were known to enjoy arguing were trying to persuade the others that it was worth pushing for their own idea of the value of an hour's ploughing. Arthur Kinsella was not one of these and he understood how valuable the extra work would be to them all. His common sense approach won the argument and they all agreed that the average of all the tenders placed was the best all round deal. Sean however, thought the 'average' price too high.

"Look friends the lowest offer was made to allow for a reasonable profit otherwise it wouldn't have been suggested, the highest was almost double this, I therefore propose offering you a deal halfway between the lowest tender and the average does that seem fair?" There was a murmur of conversation from them for a moment or two. Finally Arthur speaking for them all said

"Yes Sean we agree to your offer. When do you want us to start?"

As always seems to happen the south westerly wind on the following Saturday brought with it the heaviest rainfall of the year depositing an inch and a half by mid-day. A river of water cascaded down the roadway leading from the farm entrance to the control tower. There were very large deep puddles in the broken roadway even bigger ones were defending the entrance to the control tower.

As the party guests arrived they parked their tractors and vans on the grass as close as possible to allow passengers as short a walk as possible to avoid the worst of the driving rain. These people were country folk and were used to dealing with adverse weather conditions. A little drop of rain was infinitely better than a drought as far as they were concerned! Whilst these conditions prevailed there was nothing in the way of normal farm work that could be done, so a good time would be had enjoying the generous hospitality of the O'Reillys!

Rachel was a little concerned initially at the way the weather had turned out, she needn't have worried of course as her guests had a wonderful afternoon in the dirty neglected control tower. As evening approached, the local vicar had brought his guitar with him and he started to play some traditional Irish songs, some of the older members of the gathering knew the words and began to join in with singing.

5 8

The late summer brought with it some problems for the villagers.

They began with the unfortunate accident which caused the death of the village's only council member, Patrick Doolan who was a highly respected member of the district council and many a local person had received his help over the years. Patrick's voice was regularly heard in the council chamber offering sound advice which was often used to solve a particularly divisive problem. His passing meant the village would have to try and find a replacement if they were to enjoy representation on the council in the future.

A further problem occurred soon after Patrick Doolan's death, a mystery illness overtook the village which started with children being sent home from school suffering vomiting attacks.

Soon the disease spread through the community which worried Rachel and Sean as they were concerned for their little son. Nothing must risk his life.

Rachel washed their clothes every day and made sure everyone visiting the farm removed their footwear and washed their hands regardless of their care at home. Sean had to make trips into the village for shopping and all the other usual reasons and inevitably he went down with the violent bug. The symptoms were so bad he was unable to leave the house. He tried so hard to avoid passing the germs to Rachel and his baby son, he slept on the sofa in the living room and avoided direct contact with either of them. He had difficulty breathing, his throat was burning as though a handful of brambles was being forced down it. There was no relief whatever he tried. Drinking cold water offered only a brief respite. Please God don't let the little chap catch this horror. Three days after Sean became ill, Liam began to show signs of distress, his temperature went up to one hundred and four degrees. Dangerously high. Soon he was physically suffering with projectile vomiting. Rachel was beside herself with worry she had called the doctor who was inundated with demands for attention. Although his receptionist had promised an urgent visit it was late afternoon before he arrived at the farm.

Liam didn't cry, his breath came in short obviously extremely painful rasps.

The little body was by now very weak and looked very ill, the colour of his face had changed from a flushed redness to a pale grey. Sean and Rachel were now terrified that they were going to lose their precious heir. The doctor was extremely worried also and instructed Sean to ring for an ambulance. Liam was going to hospital. Urgently…..

59

Dublin city is a vibrant eclectic mix of individuals which made it the ideal place for Nellie Flanagan and Paddy Mc Cormick to live and work.

Their choice of occupation which had been a source of satisfaction to them both, was also a source of wealth which neither of them had planned or expected.

As a result when the money started flowing in after setting up the legal distilling of potcheen they had no idea what to do with it! The majority of the cash went straight into a joint bank account. The accidental discovery of the effect of galvanised steel on raw potcheen gave them huge pleasure as it became the most sought after in the whole of Ireland. When the old traction engine they had employed to 'enrich' the standard product finally failed it became necessary to have storage tanks specially made in Sheffield England rather than here in Ireland. They were determined to protect their secret method from their rivals.

The pair of them became famous as a result of their brew. Invitations came from the good and the shady members of Irish society. Most of these invitations were accepted and they were enjoying themselves immensely!

One day an invitation arrived from a well known high flying banker who headed his own company. This company had a string of court cases over the past few years which they had successfully defended.

Most of the events which brought them into the court were from individuals who claimed they had been swindled out of large chunks of their savings which the company was supposed to be 'looking after'.

The Chairman of the company was a charming, ruthless individual whose stock in trade was to be seen as a helpful friendly expert financier. He also had a seat on the board of a bank in Belfast which just happened to be Sean and Rachel's bank.

When Nellie and Paddy were introduced to Mr Hugh Watson they were impressed with his charm and readily invited him to visit the distillery which he in turn eagerly accepted. They all seemed to enjoy each other's company and a friendship quickly developed. Many evenings were spent together. Paddy regularly treated Hugh to dinners in one of the many superb restaurants in the city. In return he would visit the mansion home of his new friend. Nellie entertained Hugh with home cooking Irish style with her delicious beef stew and all the trimmings which he enjoyed. She also loved to give him a drop of the best ninety per cent stuff. which was totally un-molested! He loved this liquor and knew how to drink it without falling over!

"Come on Nellie, how do you produce this stuff? I promise I won't tell anyone else." He was aware that there was a 'secret' ingredient. Nellie thought he was genuinely interested in their business, she was about to talk about it when the telephone intervened....

"Hello Mum I thought I'd better give you a ring to see how you're feeling now? Sean told me you haven't been very well."

"I'm fine me darlin' 'twas only a cold so it was. I'm getting old so I am."

" Are you sure? you don't sound too good. Shall I come down to see you?"

" Well it would be very nice to see you so it would, but there's no need if you're busy which you must be with young Liam to look after. I remember what *you* were like at his age!" The conversation with Rachel went on for a few minutes more. When it ended Hugh didn't pursue his quest for knowledge of the recipe and Nellie had forgotten he'd asked.

6⊘

Rachel sat next to the incubator where Liam was fighting for his life. She was weeping quietly as she stared at the little figure lying motionless in his plastic bubble. Every few minutes a nurse came in to check his vital signs which were appearing to get weaker all the time.

Sean came into the room. He had been having a short rest after being with his son through the night. His face was drawn and lined with worry. Rachel glanced across at him as he stood beside her with tears staining his face.

"I think we're losing him Sean. The poor little mite hasn't moved at all for over an hour and he hasn't had anything to drink since we arrived." Then she too broke down and cried. Sean put his hand on her shoulder and quietly said;

"We mustn't give up yet darling we must pray for him."

"I haven't stopped praying for him since this started. We must ask the Priest to help us pray." Sean had being praying too. 'Dear God don't let us lose this one too', he thought. Presently the doctor came in and checked the baby for the umpteenth time.

"I'd like to have a word with you Mr O'Reilly on your own would be best". Rachel stared at him in alarm.

"I need to explain what happens now. Please try not to upset yourself Mrs. O'Reilly. I'm so sorry, I didn't intend to give the impression of disaster." Sean went out of the room with the consultant to get an opinion as to what was going to happen to Liam.

"I didn't want to discuss the difficulties we have regarding Liam in front of your wife at the moment. I wanted to try and discuss the prognosis with you and I have to say it doesn't look very encouraging at present. The child is having great difficulty with his breathing together with the nausea, if it carries on much longer it could lead to pneumonia.

I'm afraid if that does happen we will have to prepare ourselves for the possible loss of your son!

I'm so sorry to have to be blunt but I thought it best that you should know the situation as I see it so that you can decide whether to tell your wife." Sean was now frightened at the prospect of not only losing Liam but the effect this would have on his darling Rachel. He was now burdened with too much knowledge…. How was he going to go back into that ward without displaying his feeling of devastation?

When he did return to her side she searched his face for any signs which would give away his distress and confirm her own. Sean did his best to appear hopeful with the smile he gave her, it was apparent that she had not allowed herself to consider the possibility of losing the little boy. Instead she returned his smile for which he was grateful. He was not ready yet to repeat what he had been told. There was nothing to be gained from causing her any unnecessary anguish. Right now it was time to pray again.

Sean held Rachel's hand.

"I think it's time we called Nellie to let her know how things are sweetheart. I know she's beside herself with worry right now."

Sean realised the situation required delicate handling, he knew that Nellie wanted to be near her family in spirit at this frightening time.

"Yes Sean, you're right of course, you do it please. Give her my love.

61

Hugh Watson was enjoying an evening of rural Irish entertainment with Paddy. They were both well lubricated by the time he got round to posing the question which had remained un-answered by Nellie Flanagan.

"That best stuff of yours Paddy, I've never tasted anything like it before, how come its so different from all the others?"

"Well Hugh we took ages to make the original sample. We tried dozens of different mixes before we found the perfect recipe." Paddy liked their posh friend but there was no way he would disclose their secret. He wouldn't have given his old ma the secret, God bless her soul. To avoid any disagreement he used the gift bestowed on him at Castle Blarney and confused his companion with half an hour's worth of mythical ingredients without any mention of scaffolding or galvanized storage.

The distillery was now dispatching one thousand bottles of the enriched product to an agent in Tokyo every month. A convoy of lorries were on the ferry from Dublin to Glasgow and a similar delivery existed to England via Cardiff! All thanks to a load of old pipes! A regular private customer was collecting his 'Special' version on a regular basis. This gentleman was never asked for any payment, by chance he happened to work for the Customs as its inspector of distilleries!

62

The four days Liam had hung on to life seemed an eternity. Rachel and Sean had had very little sleep between them. On the morning of the fifth day the night shift had just gone off duty. One of the day nurses came into the side room where Liam had fought so hard and approached the sleeping baby. His cheeks were looking almost the right colour and he had stopped wheezing. His breathing was slow and steady and his eyes were now open. The nurse turned off the oxygen supply and removed the plastic dome which had covered him as he lay so near death only the day before.

Rachel was asleep in her chair whilst this was happening, she felt the light touch of the nurse's hand on her shoulder and woke with a start.

Staring wide eyed up at the nurse she was half expecting to be told bad news. Instead she was looking into the smiling face of the delighted young nurse whose pleasant task was now to tell her that her little boy had finally come through.

Liam was alive!

"Sean, he's come through! He's made it! Thank God he's made it!"

Rachel cried as she told him on the phone. The Aston Martin burnt a lot of rubber as it carried the boy's father to the hospital to be with him and his relieved mother.

Nothing they could say would convey adequately their gratitude to the doctor and nurses for their care which had saved Liam. There was nothing the hospital staff could say to them either, which could show the relief they all felt at this wonderful outcome.

Carrying him to the car in his carry cot later, Rachel noticed how light it now felt. Obviously he had lost a great deal of weight during those awful, frightful days. It would be Rachel's pleasant task to ensure the child's body weight increased rapidly.

Following the harrowing events at the hospital, many of their friends made a point of telling them how they had prayed for the positive outcome which had occurred. The warm feeling they had each time one of these lovely people reached out to them with simple words of kindness and encouragement was wonderful.

When Rachel rang Nellie to give her the news of Liam's recovery she was grateful for her mother's obvious relief. The tone in Nellie's words conveyed far more than the words themselves.

"I'll be on the bus first thing in the morning darlin' girl. You'll both be needin' a rest. I'll take over for a few days so as you can catch up on some sleep."

This was one of those times when Rachel realised the important part her mother played in their lives and she treasured the thought.

"Thanks mum. We'd like that."

63

Arthur Kinsella arrived on the doorstep of the bungalow a couple of days after Liam's safe return.

"Mornin Sean. I hope you don't mind me droppin in like this?"

"Of course not Arthur, you're always welcome. What can I do for you?"

"It's really a question of what you can do for all of us in the village really."

"Oh, how's that?"

"Well, as you know with the loss of poor old Patrick we have no representation on the council. Some of the boys have asked me to see if you would stand as a candidate in the election?"

Sean had a puzzled frown on his face when the two men ended their conversation, he was a farmer wasn't he? what did he know of politics? Some serious thought would have to be given to the matter before he could decide whether to accede to this invitation.

"What's up?" Rachel asked as Sean came into the room.

"They want me to stand as the candidate at the election next month. What do you think love, should we have a go?"

"Well, if the villagers want you to do it they must have discussed the idea.

Why not see if they are prepared to help with door to door canvassing and whatever?" Between them Sean and Rachel decided that they would like to be able to represent their friends from the farms and the village on the council.

64

Something had been bothering Nellie regarding the enquiring nature of the conversations she'd been having with Hugh Fraser.

"Paddy?"

"Yep Nell. What's up?"

"I know you like Hugh don't you?"

"So.?"

"Do you trust him?

"Why? Don't you?"

"I'm not too sure. I do get on with him , he makes me laugh."

"Well, something is obviously bothering you about him isn't it?"

"He asked me the other day how we make the best stuff."

"You didn't tell him Nell did you?"

"No, of course not. I almost did though."

"What stopped you?"

"The phone did!"

"How's that?"

"Rachel phoned just after he asked me that day, she wanted to talk.

Afterwards I think he'd forgotten. Anyway, he didn't ask again."

"Why would a wealthy banker be interested in the basics of brewing potcheen do you reckon? As a matter of fact he asked me for the recipe too!"

The two of them now realised that their friend was up to something and it probably wasn't in their interest. Caution would be their watchword from now on.

The demand was so great for their product that it was proving difficult to provide adequate supplies.

Sean was brought into the discussions about plans for the future. It was obvious that serious changes were going to have to be made if all clients were to be satisfied. The special meeting of its three shareholders took place at Nellie's apartment in Dublin.

This was such a prosperous business that they decided to hold their get-together in private. No prying eyes or busy ears to get wind of their future plans were going to be present. The meeting was totally informal as they wanted maximum input from everyone. Nellie opened the meeting by pouring everyone a glass of 'special'.

"Enjoy it. It's the only one you're having until the meeting's over!" she announced. They all agreed that they must stay sober to discuss the business in hand.

"The job is too big for just the two of us to handle now." Paddy declared.

"We're making a fortune and that's lovely but we have to be working seven days a week to keep up with all the paper work. The brewing side is easy, we can just keep taking on more workers. With all the transport organising and invoicing, receipts and delivery notes to be checked not to mention the tax returns and all."

"So what you're saying is you need a secretary or two isn't that the answer?" queried Sean.

"Yes, if you're not bothered about the competition getting wind of what we're up to." answered Nellie.

"You don't need to give any information about the formula to anyone else do you. It would be a question of any new employees just doing the job you give them wouldn't it?" Sean responded.

"We have a client who has become very friendly to both of us, a very nice guy who is a big noise in the bank. This chap wants to treat us to slap up meals and concerts. Even offered me a free holiday on his private yacht in the Caribbean!" Paddy declared.

"What have you had to do for those kinds of favours Paddy?"

"That's just it Sean, absolutely nothing except keep him in hooch. The special stuff."

"What's this man's name. I'll try and find out something about him. If he's on the level I'd take him up on his holiday offer!"

The meeting went on late into the night. After much discussion it was decided to advertise for a competent book keeper / secretary as the only possible solution beyond selling the business to a rival which was an absolute 'no' to them all. Having seen the books and been on the receiving end of generous dividend payments Sean could understand their reticence.

The turnover was extraordinary. It was obvious that none of them would ever be short of the better things in life, one of which was the amazing 'special' version of potcheen, and no one else was going to have the formula for that!

The next morning Sean had a discussion with Bill Fraser in an attempt to find out a little about Paddy and Nellie's friend, Mr Hugh Watson. Bill confessed that he had never heard of him, but would make some enquiries to try to identify Paddy's mysterious benefactor.

Sean had been having a few thoughts of his own as to the future of the distillery. Although it wouldn't be a popular idea with his fellow directors, it might be getting near the time to think about 'going Public' and floating the company on the London Stock Exchange, if such a move was possible. It would probably necessitate the head office being sited up in the Province. Enquiries would be made. Those enquiries began with contacting his good friend Bill.

If he could do plenty of research before confronting Nellie and Paddy and if the sums looked good and they wouldn't have to give up their overall control of the business they might allow the idea to progress. A large handful of 'ifs'.

Sean was keen to relieve himself of his involvement. There was enough to think about with the coming election so he would have to take a back seat anyway. Particularly if he was the successful candidate. Bill was, as usual, helpful with his advice. The experts in the city would have to have access to all the companies' records and would be all over them 'like a rash', but the advantages of 'going public' were probably well worth those inconvenient meddlers from the city scrutinising the distillery. Sean knew he would have to put together a very convincing package if he was going to have any hope of persuading Nell that she would be happy with the outcome. Paddy he was sure, would be more pragmatic.

65

The business projects on the airport were now well established although the pig trade was no longer profitable, the effluent supply was still being used in the compost business.

The fertiliser company was increasing its turnover every year. Mick's Mix was registered as a limited company. Huge quantities of 'Raw Material' were delivered from all over the country including the use of large tankers for the collection of the liquid version which was still essential for the finished article.

There were still some empty buildings on the farm which were suitable for various small business projects. Sean was now actively seeking tenants for them. It hadn't been possible to lease these out when the aerodrome belonged to the British government but as he now owned the whole site there was no longer any restriction. Within a week of the advert appearing in the local paper there were several interesting responses.

Out of town supermarkets were now springing up all over Britain. These in turn created a demand for products which had hitherto been classified as 'luxury' items. Chicken was no longer regarded as a special food only available to the wealthy for the Sunday roast. Production of poultry products had increased dramatically during the seventies. Producers now needed premises for intensive rearing and processing. Specialist restaurants needed a constant supply of young birds to satisfy demand. It was therefore, no surprise that almost as soon as the news was out that sheds and paddocks were available to rent at the aerodrome, applications by post and phone were arriving at Sean's office. An interesting call came from a large motor car dealer who was in need of a covered area to store new vehicles after shipment from the UK prior to dispersal around both the Province and Eire showrooms. There were three hangars on the site. Two were already in use as straw and fodder stores, these would be ideal and so were let at very acceptable rates.

Within the month most of the available buildings, sheds and previously vacant open areas were let. The aerodrome had become an industrial site, the income from which was better than owning a mint! It was now obvious that the pig farm was no longer viable, as most pig products consumed in the British Isles were of Danish origin. Profit had completely disappeared. There was a cost problem with the Mick's Mix product also as more and more farmers were using chemical fertilizers. Without the slurry available on site if the pig farm ceased production, there would be no need for the distribution of the smelly bi-product!

Sean and Rachel were facing the dilemma of finding worthwhile employment for their loyal staff. They were determined to return this loyalty whatever the cost. The quality of all of these people would make this a challenging task. In the event it turned out to be easier than expected. Sheila had already approached the owner of a poultry unit and was immediately hired as manager.

Mickey was disappointed that his factory was under threat of closure and many evenings were spent trying to convince his employers that there was a future for Mick's Mix. Sean was eventually able to convince him that the time was past and that they must 'move on'.

"Look son, if you can find another marketable product which needs packing in large paper bags fine, I'll support you, if not we'll find something else for you. I'll give you a month. If you haven't put together a viable business plan by then I'm afraid we'll just shut the plant down."

Sean was blunt with Mickey about the end of another business. He had to be as these were difficult times. A recession was looming and unless the weaker elements were dealt with before they became major loss makers they could very easily become a serious problem.

Early financial difficulties with the awful Jones at the bank had taught Sean to be pragmatic. Bill was the catalyst in his new attitude and Sean was aware of it. Now was the time to approach his old friend, who was nearing early retirement at the bank, to join him officially as a director of the burgeoning business empire.

"Hi Bill, how about we all go out for dinner at the weekend? I've something I'd like to discuss with you."

"Sounds good Sean, I'll just have a word with the head gardener and ring you back. OK?"

Soon it was agreed that they would enjoy one of their pleasant soirees. It was always a pleasant diversion from normal activity to go out with Bill and Jane. Rachel and Jane were regular co-shoppers and an evening out would give Rachel a chance to arrange another session with her friend. They had their usual table by the window of their favourite restaurant. As was their custom, the evening began with choosing the wine. Over the years Sean had learned quite a lot about wine and was good at picking ones which they all enjoyed.

After the usual small talk, children, the weather etcetera Sean brought up the subject which had prompted this rendezvous.

"Rachel and I want to make a proposal to you Bill."

"Go ahead, I'm all ears."

"Well, do you remember our discussion about the development of the airfield just after we bought it?"

"Vaguely, yes. I remember throwing some ideas at you afterwards."

"The point is Bill, things are developing at a hectic gallop. With this recession developing we really need to find as much profitable use as possible for the airfield. The domestic site is almost completely let now as you know, but there must be ways to profit from the rest of the place."

" Of course there is Sean. John Shepherd is always carping on to me about it."

"Such as.?"

"He is really keen to use the runways but won't tell me what for."

"Well Bill, Rachel and I have been talking and wonder if you were serious when you said you wouldn't mind joining our company officially. As you're soon reaching early retirement. How about it?" Bill looked across the table at Jane who seemed a little uneasy. Plans had already formed in her mind as to Bill's retirement and its aftermath. Bill was silent for a moment or two as though he was searching for the words to decline the proposal.

"It's a great idea Sean. I'll have to think about it though. Please give me a day or two and in the meantime perhaps you could let me have an idea of what my role would be?"

"I'll write to you with as much info. as I can. Including financial inducement!"

The rest of the evening continued with the usual banter between friends.

Sean spent the whole of that Sunday trying to think of specific tasks for Bill if he joined them. Throwing suggestions to Rachel as she went about cooking their lunch.

"Why not just give him the job of general advisor and financial director?" she suggested.

"Of course! That is precisely what we're looking for isn't it?"

The draft letter he wrote was very short. It simply said 'Dear Bill, we want your on-going advice on a day to day basis with special responsibility for finance. Your salary obviously negotiable. Just give us an indication of your expectation in this regard. Yours etcetera.

When he read the letter Bill Fraser was relieved. At last his plan was becoming reality. It had taken them long enough to realise they needed him.

Sean and Rachel had to go down to Dublin on a visit to 'Kilmona Whiskey Distilleries'. Nellie and Paddy wanted to discuss marketing strategy with them.

Sean's suggestion that the company be floated as a public concern was not a popular one as he suspected and communication between himself and Paddy was rude, short and generally unpleasant. Paddy liked being the boss and didn't see the point of shareholders questioning his judgement. They might even think they could *tell* him what to do! Oh no. Not a good idea at all. Sean knew he was going to have a real battle to get his way on this.

"It's OK right *now* Paddy." Sean postulated.

"But in a couple of years time you'll be what, forty eight years old? You, like the rest of us, will get old one day and that will be sooner than you think. And there's a recession coming. We need new ideas, new thinking."

"To be sure I'll be old some day Sean and probably thicker than I am now, but remember this. 'Twas meself who found the secret of the good stuff was it not? and me and Nell who started this place was in not?

"Of course all of that is true Paddy, I could also argue that none of what you've done would have been possible without Rachel's and my hard earned cash! None of this is relevant. We have got to face facts if we all want what's best for the company".

The arguments flowed back and forth until they were almost shouting at each other. To end the stalemate Rachel suggested they should ask the advice of Nell and Paddy's good friend the bank executive chap. This seemed an acceptable compromise to the warring pair.

"We'll leave it up to you Paddy, to have a word with, what's his name?"

"Hugh Watson."

"Yes. Mister Watson. Will you accept his advice on this?"

Reluctantly Paddy agreed.

It was only a couple of days after this that Sean received a reply from Bill following their invitation, agreeing to the proposal with gratitude and pleasure.

Jane was easily convinced that this was an opportunity that Bill should accept. She knew the moment Sean and Rachel had suggested it that her own plans were easily discarded. Her man's future was far more important to her. Bill also wanted to do this desperately, but it had been important to discuss it with his wife before accepting.

66

All the villagers and farmers were as good as their word when it was time to start canvassing for the council election. A meeting was arranged in the new community hall. Any volunteers to assist Mister O'Reilly in his candidacy would be very welcome the advert said. The response was overwhelming. The hall was crammed with whole families who wanted to help.

This was a wonderful community. Rachel volunteered to be co-ordinator for the election. Posters were designed and printed by a local artist. Rosettes were also chosen and pamphlets with Sean's manifesto were produced and an army of distributors was elected to distribute these to every house and farm on the electoral list. Sean concentrated on speech making and visiting businesses in the area. This election was a full time occupation until the result was known.

The election turned out to be an exciting affair with two other candidates scrambling for votes. One of these was a young woman who represented Sinn Fein, the other was a bellicose young man with red hair who was standing for the official Unionist party. In the event, Sean was elected with an overwhelming majority over the other candidates who went out of their way to congratulate him. This duty was to become a very important part of his life.

The 'troubles' in the province meant hardship for most of the population. The British army was everywhere, trying mostly unsuccessfully to maintain order. Attempting to segregate the religious extremists. The sound of explosives going off was a regular occurrence in the city of Belfast. These were extremely difficult times. Sean had to deal with many sectarian complaints as a councillor. Rarely was he successful in solving the difficult problems presented to him which were of a sectarian nature.

He was seen though by most as a fair and wise councillor. The projects on the airfield itself were progressing slowly. Care had to be taken on every decision they made. Making enemies of one side or the other had to be avoided as mindless retribution would surely follow any contentious issue.

With this background it was a cautious Bill who approached his chairman Sean, with the idea of using the airfield for what it was originally intended. "What do you have in mind Bill, bearing in mind the prevention of terrorism laws with all the mandatory regulations which accompanies those ?"

"I've now been approached officially by John Shepherd to examine the possibility of using the runway for private flying. He has his own aircraft and wants to use our field as his base in Ireland."

"I very much doubt the British government would allow it Bill. Without a huge amount of investment with security around the perimeter. The purchase and erection of fencing, floodlights etcetera not to mention setting up a professional Air traffic control system and so on. However Bill, you'd better make enquiries and see what is involved."

Sean couldn't understand why Belfast City airport or Aldergrove couldn't be used for Mister Shepherd's base. Cost obviously wasn't a factor if John Shepherd owned his own aircraft. Bill first contacted the CAA to find out what their requirements were before going into the other legalities. What fun!

Investigating the possibility of opening up flying activity on the airfield was not as onerous as they expected. The CAA had a few objections of a technical nature which were easily met. The police were only concerned initially, with the requirement that Special Branch be informed before any aircraft landed or took off so that security checks could be maintained constantly. Extra perimeter fences were not required, not yet anyway. Bill was pleased to be able to go back to his old boss with this positive information. John Shepherd was even more pleased to receive the news, in fact he was delighted.

A board meeting was due to take place at the farm on November eleventh the farm's official year's end. This was the time tenant farmers usually dreaded.

Rent was due and all the year's outstanding invoices from the farm supplies firms had to be settled. The usual people were present. Sean and Rachel, Sheila, Mickey, their accountant Joe Kennish and bank manager Simon Forbes. Bill was introduced as the new company director formally taking his place for the first time. The minutes had been issued the previous day and so were taken as read, then the proposals for the next twelve months were given which were received with mixed feelings by some of those present. Sheila and Mickey were losing their present jobs. Sheila would not be attending any more of these gatherings as her new job was with a different firm.

Mickey had no idea where the next year would take him. Sean had, but it would wait until another day.

Sean had almost forgotten that he had asked Bill to find out about Hugh Watson, Nellie and Paddy's rich buddy, when Bill announced that he'd had a word with John Shepherd to see if he could shed any light on this character.

John had come back to him saying he had heard of Hugh, he is a high flyer in banking circles but keeps quiet about his activities. Apparently he's a 'Hedge' fund manager. " One of those people who buy shares in companies who do well, then when the shares rise in value sell them on at a profit. Some do very well others not so well. And some are bent as a hairpin as my old mum used to say!"

"Which category does he think this Hugh Watson fits?" asked Sean.

"Dunno he didn't say."

"Any chance of finding out Bill? If he is a crook they need to be on their guard down there."

"I'll make some further enquiries. I have a few other contacts in the bank and my stock-broker may be able to help. Anyway leave it with me for a few days.

Sean was feeling a little un-easy about this man. Why would someone like him behave in such a generous way for a few bottles of Whiskey? It rang alarm bells.

He was somewhat surprised at Paddy's reluctance to consider the possibility of 'going Public'. It would mean a lucrative early retirement if he chose to sell his share of the business. No matter, there was not going to be a war over it. Nellie was all for the idea though which *was* a surprise! She was in her eighties now so probably too tired to carry on as they had been these last few years.

Hugh Watson came visiting soon after Paddy's disagreement with Sean. This was a good opportunity to quiz his knowledgeable friend about Sean's idea.

"Say Hugh, Sean reckons it would be a good idea to float the company on the London Stock Exchange. What d'you reckon?"

"Paddy, if I were you I wouldn't dream of doing such a thing at the moment.

Maybe in a year or two after the coming recession has run its course."

"Could you give me a note to that effect for me to give him? I doubt he'd believe me without that."

"Sure, no problem. I'll do it right away. Give me a piece of paper from the office." Paddy noticed the copperplate handwriting. How distinguished it looked. He knew that Sean would realise that it was authentic because of the quality of the script and the prose itself. He folded it carefully and placed it in an envelope which had the company's logo printed on the reverse. After sealing it he stamped it and put it in the pile of mail for posting.

It occurred to him as he licked the gum on the envelope how quickly the time was passing, it seemed only a couple of years since he and Sean were banged-up together. Now they were discussing retirement! There were times though he knew he was getting on in years and that someday he would *have* to think seriously about giving up. Not today though.

67

Nell wasn't her usual self when Paddy called her to fill her in with the gist of his conversation with Hugh and he was quite worried. Nellie Flanagan wasn't one to be ill, no germs had dared approach her in all her years. A regular consumption of potcheen made sure of that! Paddy was so concerned that he decided to pop round to her apartment to check that she was OK.

When he knocked on her door and got no answer he tried calling her name through her letter box. Still no answer. He tried the door which opened , calling her name as he went, he got no response. Eventually he found her unconscious on the floor of her kitchen. She was very cold and appeared not to be breathing.

Paddy frantically dialled for an ambulance and waited anxiously for the arrival of medical assistance. When the ambulance staff checked her out it was obvious that Nellie had gone to the 'hooch home in the sky'. She had died as she had lived, with a gentle smile on her lips and still wearing her gold rimmed spectacles!

Nell's passing was the end of an era. Her legacy was still being enjoyed by her clients across the globe. When Rachel was told of Nellie's passing she wished she had spent more time with her mother. They were so different. Their worlds were alien to each other, in a strange way it was because they were so different she wished she and her family *had* shared more of their lives with her. Now it was too late. She was gone. The funeral was organised according to her wishes.

The coffin was made from local pine from the forest at Kilmona, this was placed in the galvanised whiskey tank in Dublin. The request asked that the casket be immersed for a day and a night in the precious liquid! Enough time to impregnate the wood prior to being used to contain her remains. If there *was* life after death she wanted to take the wonderful flavour with her!

The 'guests' at her wake were to send her off in style with toasts using the 'best stuff '! Among those attending was a retired police sergeant named Roger Casey and a small, stooped bald headed old man who turned out to be a retired friendly Customs Inspector!

These were specially invited at Nellie's request in a note she had left to be opened immediately after her demise. The coffin was carried to the church on a brewer's dray, the humour wasn't lost on anyone. Nellie Flanagan deceased, knew it wouldn't be!

Following Nellie's death Rachel inherited her share of the distillery, another of her jokes, knowing how much Rachel hated the whole hooch business. The sum involved was very considerable. Paddy knew that he would have to find the cash to buy out her share somehow, if she was prepared to part with it. Poor Paddy, he'd still not been able to repair the damage to his friendship with Sean following their disagreement over the future of the business. Now he would *have* to!

68

The call from Simon Forbes following Sean's request for a statement on his current account declared;

"I think you need to move some of this into an investment of some sort Sean. There's far too much in the account for comfort."

"Are you telling me it isn't safe Simon?"

"No. Of course not, but you are getting very little interest in a current account".

"Well, what do you advise me to do?"

"I think you need to talk to a qualified financial advisor. May I suggest one or two?"

"Please."

Rachel seemed very pleased with herself Sean thought, she had just come into the house from a shopping trip with Jane. "Why the smug grin darling. I take it you had some satisfactory therapy in the city?"

"Oh yes! Jane helped me choose the new dining room furniture. You'll love it Sean. Light oak table with two leaves so that we'll have plenty of room to seat eight for dinner! with eight high back leather chairs. Matching sideboard and corner cabinet for booze and glasses. Next time we go shopping it'll be the lounge stuff!"

This was fun, listening to her plans for their new home. The building had taken a long time, much longer than the last time. But then, this house was so much bigger. Rachel was enjoying herself immensely. With the last house, on the aerodrome, money was very tight and they had to 'make do' with all their old furniture. Liam was a baby then too!

With the excitement of all this going on Sean hadn't noticed Rachel getting up earlier than usual and disappearing into the bathroom. The sickness she felt was put down to all the extra activity in her life After a week of this nauseous feeling she began to wonder if she aught to pay a visit to the doctor. She decided to have a quiet word with a nurse friend who she often met on her walks to the village.

"It's been going on for about ten days, otherwise I'm fine." Rachel told her.

"Sounds to me like you'd better get the pram out again love. I reckon you're pregnant!"

And so she was. After seeing the doctor it was confirmed. Three weeks or so was his estimate. Rachel was overjoyed at her condition and it was an equally delighted Sean after being given the happy news. Bill arrived at the house soon after Sean was told he was going to be a father again. "That's terrific news Sean. Perhaps now is the best time to consider furthering those investment plans. I've made a note of a couple of advisers and contact details for you as I promised."

Sean decided to contact the first name on the list Bill gave him. 'Horton Associates-Financial Services' senior partner, Thomas Horton. A meeting was arranged for Sean to discuss his needs with a Mister D Jones, who would be delighted to assist.

Another Mr Jones to deal with. Surely this character couldn't compete with 'the other one' for assinide stupidity. Could he? The thought left Sean's brain as quickly as it had entered. Once the present decision regarding investments had been satisfactorily concluded it might be possible to eradicate all thoughts of the name 'Jones' being synonymous with stupidity!

Bill was of course right, investment had to be made to ensure the best possible home for the growing family fortune. The amount of cash sitting lazily in the current account was getting larger every week.

Rachel probably wouldn't be quite as keen on the idea as Sean was. She'd been able to happily indulge in her 'hobby' of retail therapy without a second thought as to where the cash was coming from.

It was going to be a sticky few minutes after he informed her that she was going to have to revert to budgeting.

To soften the blow she could have a quick blast on the credit card before her allowance would be implemented!

69

Rachel's latest pregnancy was presenting no problems until she went to the maternity clinic for the usual scan. The scan presented a surprise with the evidence of two images. She was going to have twins! The parents were ecstatic at this revelation and were eager to spread the news to share their delight.

Twins. What a delightful situation was developing. Rachel had revelled in motherhood with young Liam.

The idea of two more children around their house was exciting.

Maybe a little brother and sister for Liam. Even two girls would be nice. Shopping for two little girls would make their mum a very happy one!

Speculation, although pointless, was fun. Sean could visualise having to buy one of those new-fangled two seater prams. Car seats would need to be purchased also. If two girls arrived they would have to have separate rooms eventually. He knew from his experience with his wife that the female variety of human, demanded an enormous amount of cupboard space and knick-knack shelves for 'essentials' and cupboards for all their stange clothes. Not to mention the bottles and tubes of war paint. Hair drying and styling equipment. Dozens of pairs of shoes and of course, photograph frames to display images of their favourite spotty faced pop stars!

Of course it hadn't happened yet. They might be two boys. All they would need was a couple of bunk beds and room in the garage for their bikes!

70

It was in high spirits that Sean went for his appointment with the financial expert Bill had recommended as his new advisor.

It came as somewhat of a surprise when ushered into the plush office, to recognise the face and diminutive frame of the one individual who was not likely to instil a shed-full of confidence in him. Sean stood and stared in total disbelief.

What on earth was Bill thinking of? Recommending Derek, Mister disaster Jones. Ex bank manager! There *had* to be a mistake. This was the man who couldn't understand the basic principles of banking. Now he was beckoning Sean to take a seat in this plush palace of wealth! *No way.* He was speechless with astonishment, and stood rooted to the spot to recover his composure. Eventually he turned on his heel and left the office in disgust.

It was unbelievable. Jones again! There was absolutely no way he was going to allow that creep to 'advise' him on money matters or any   other subject come to that.

"Thanks for arranging the meeting at Horton's for me Bill. Did you know that the delightful Mr Jones is their number one adviser?"

"I hope you're joking Sean. I know that he's been on courses for investment, but I wouldn't have thought he would have been accepted by Tom Horton. I'm so sorry. It must have been embarrassing for you."

"No Bill, *I* wasn't embarrassed but I made damn sure *he* was!

Needless to say I didn't stay long enough to get any advice."

Bill was furious when Sean told him what had happened.

PART TWO ⊕

1991....

7 1

The name on his office door said Philip Baverstock. There was no reason for anyone in the building to suspect the dapper, eloquent man who occasionally visited the place wasn't who he said he was. In fact this was only one of his aliases. Victor Harvey was a clever, smooth operator who knew his way around the fiscal world. There was no secret corner he hadn't discovered over the last forty seven years in the business. Starting his working life as a junior filing clerk in the bank's headquarters in Belfast.

Victor had always been clever, even at school he always had money in his pocket when his peers had to use their spare time from schoolwork doing chores to earn pocket money. There was always a scheme he could exploit. People, he realised when a very young man, were gullible. As such they deserved to be used to provide him with his 'disposable' income. Most of his *scams* were perpetrated on people who trusted him and didn't know anything about him or where he lived. It was always important to him to charm his 'target' first. Using a false name he behaved in a 'Walter Mitty' fashion whilst operating. It was this skill at subterfuge which propelled his career in the banking profession.

Victor's skill as a con-man catapulted him into the stratosphere of the successful boardroom directorships which enabled him to become a very wealthy man indeed. His activities made others wealthy too, which of course, made him some influential friends. It would also make him some very determined enemies…

"Derek, I want you to go to the Staff College and get yourself enrolled on the financial adviser course."

He was speaking to Derek Jones who had been removed from management way back in the sixties as being unsympathetic to clients. Since he was moved to Head Office he had become a very useful 'mover and shaker', provided he was steered in the right direction! Whenever any of the directors had an awkward job to do, when a client was difficult or a slightly dodgy contract was needed dealing with, Jones' manner came in handy diverting attention away from his boss. Whoever that was at the time.

"Yes Sir. When do you want me to go?"

"Find out when the next session starts and get on with it."

Derek Jones was also a creep. A 'yes' man…. Jolly useful!

It was obvious in view of his past history upsetting valuable customers he would have to be monitored for some time before he would be allowed to offer any further advice.

Jones' time at head office had reined him in. John Shepherd had given him a hard time and brain-washed him into his own way of thinking. Up to a point….

A newly trained 'advisor' equipped with all the latest thinking was hopefully, another way of steering clients in the right direction as far as the bank was concerned. All John Shepherd had to do was hope the course was effective.

72

Paddy reluctantly grasped the nettle after considering the alternatives for his own future, hoping his decision wouldn't jump up and sting him later and called Sean to talk about the idea of 'going public' with the distillery. It was a damn shame though. He'd resisted this action for so many years. Now seemed the right time, but passing on the secret of the 'Best Stuff' to someone else didn't seem right. Nell would turn in her grave if the secret is lost!

"Yes Paddy of course we can talk, whenever you like." Sean replied to the quest for discussion on what had been a sore subject between them.

"Right Sean I'll see you tomorrow then so I will. At your place, ten o'clock." At last Sean could see a possible ending to the hooch saga. These had been such a wasteful few years. Time to sort Paddy out once and for all and get shot of the blasted distillery! Rachel would be delighted.

After mending the badly splintered verbal fences, Sean and Paddy continued the meeting at the Foamin' Ferkin over lunch.

"So how do we go about getting the old hooch factory listed, or whatever?"

"Well Paddy, first of all we need to find a suitable broker who can set the wheels in motion. It will take quite a time as the relevant authorities have to research the business to establish its suitability for flotation. This could take many months.

"OK I'm in no hurry. I'll be sorry to lose control of it though Sean, particularly the 'Special'. I really don't want to watch some city bloke picking up bonuses every year on our little fiddle!"

"I'll get in touch with Joe, Joe Kennish the accountant and Simon Forbes.

Simon's an investment consultant now, those two can go to the Stock exchange in London to get the low down on procedure. I understand they do courses which give a thorough insight into the workings of the exchange. They also advise on what to expect after being listed on their Main Market. Their rules are very tight so you'd better make sure that the financial side of the business is absolutely 'spot on' before we get started. Right?"

"I'll get on to it right away. And Sean, thanks for everything."

This course was different from the one Derek Jones was attending. This one promised to be useful to all concerned. The O'Reilly/Flanagan/McCormick potcheen consortium in particular.

This was going to be the starting point of an entirely new era. Having decided to go ahead with the flotation of the distillery Paddy wanted to see the job done as quickly as possible. He was going to pass the mantle of responsibility to a bunch of faceless city bods after all these years.

He knew it was going to be a traumatic event which he would have to endure for a while. The best way of coping would be to make a complete break and move back to the Province to seek a new, less demanding challenge. Perhaps Rachel and Sean could use a hand with one of their charities?

2000

73

When the twins were born, Rachel and Sean decided on popular English names for them, they were both boys. The eldest, by five minutes was Michael who weighed in at a hefty eight pounds six ounces was chubby with fair hair. Sean looked at him with a quizzical gaze. Everyone on both sides of the family had very dark hair! Jonathan was blessed with a thick head of black hair and was somewhat dainty. He weighed only five pounds and a couple of ounces. Both the babies were fit and healthy though and put on weight rapidly. As the twins grew up it was Jonathan who filled out to be the biggest and strongest of the two of them.

Michael suited his blond hair and deep blue eyes! The boys both excelled academically at their boarding school. Jonathon was athletic in build and became a very good sportsman captaining his house and school at rugby. Michael was artistic and was active at drama, taking the male lead in all the school productions. These gifted boys both gained entrance to University at Cambridge. Jonathan studied law and politics. Michael read accountancy and information technology. On graduating Jonathan was articled to a large criminal lawyer's practice before being called to the Bar.

Michael became a successful accountant prior to realising his ambition to become an actuary.

With another lawyer and an accountant in the family this was a formidable team in the business world and all three boys headed by Liam, were destined to manage the family cluster of businesses. Sean and Rachel encouraged their sons in their business interests which would undoubtedly be an advantage in their future careers .

Sean had been extremely fortunate in most of his business dealings, the majority of which were financially successful. These businesses were run by carefully selected managers.

The central core of the empire was still the aerodrome and the interests which developed as a result of the buildings which the RAF had needed for its wartime activity. The airfield itself had been extensively developed as a private airport, mainly used for the developing holiday package trade. A few private pilots used the strip for pleasure flying but mostly the activity was of a commercial nature and was very profitable. Sean had gained his private pilot's licence and kept a small twin engined machine for his many trips to London when business demanded his presence.

As the years passed, Rachel and Sean had become involved in many charitable works, Rachel devoting her energy to children's needs generally, but also the local community benefited from her tireless energy whenever the need arose. Sean found himself involved in the business world, helping young people to get employment both in Ireland and all over England and Wales.

It came as a surprise to both of them when the letter arrived from the Prime Minister's office to inform Sean that he was to receive the OBE for his service to youth welfare. The local community was delighted when the news became official and decided to organise a party for their popular patron.

A very proud family journeyed to London for the investiture. Sean was visibly nervous before being ushered in to meet the Queen to receive his award.

74

Following Bill Fraser's advice, Sean agreed to make another appointment with the financial advisers who employed Derek Jones. He waited for the individual sitting on the other side of the ultra modern desk to open the dialogue between them. This, thought Sean, was going to be either a difficult long winded sermon which their ancient history would suggest, or it was going to be the shortest interview he had ever heard of!

In the event this 'new' Derek Jones seemed to have mellowed over the intervening years which put Sean on his guard as never before!

"It's *so* nice to see you again after all these years," he said in a totally patronising way. Sean didn't respond to this insincere opening. He couldn't find the words to fit his incredulity at the situation he found himself in. All he could do was nod his head at the little figure who was now grinning at him.

"I understand you'd like some help with some investments?"

Sean regained his composure before responding;

"Forgive me if I seem a little puzzled Mr Jones. The last time we met you were not exactly my biggest fan were you?"

"I admit we had a few problems Mr O'Reilly, but I always had your welfare in mind. Small farmers always tried to borrow far more money than their business could possibly afford. Most of the ones I dealt with went bankrupt."

"So correct me if I'm wrong, what you're saying is that no small farmer could ever progress to better himself regardless of the business potential of his farm?

That there is no point in looking beyond each day's bank figure.? Tomorrow doesn't count, or matter as far as you're concerned. Now you're sitting across this desk from me, suggesting I should seriously take notice of *your* advice?"

"Please Mr O'Reilly!" Jones spluttered as he pleaded with Sean to listen to his appeal for understanding. "It's a long time since I moved on from being your bank manager and I suspect we've both learned a lot since those days. You should realise that banking has changed a good deal since then. The present thinking is to lend as much as possible to practically anyone who wants it!

Ever since Maggie decided that council houses should be disposed of, preferably to the sitting tenant, regardless of whether he could afford the repayments or not, the profligate lending by the banks and building societies has escalated ever since."

"I am very aware of that. Give me credit for a little intelligence. I've had to assist so many people in my life because of that stupidity." Sean could feel his pent up aggression welling up. It would be so easy to really lose his temper.

After all the lectures he had endured from the 'expert' sitting opposite him he was now expected to listen to this tripe.

Quickly regaining his self control he used the meeting as a chance to reverse roles, and teach this ignoramus a thing or two about financial prudence! Remaining on his feet to give him extra height over his unfortunate target, he continued;

"It's pretty obvious that you are not qualified to advise grannies to suck eggs Mr Jones. It is basic common sense that if you lend one hundred and twenty per cent of the value of a property based on six and a half years earned income is an insane policy. It cannot possibly be maintained. A hiccough in the economy across the country will cause substantial unemployment and the whole financial pyramid will likely come crashing down!

You bankers if that happens will be entirely responsible. Do you realise that?"

"Oh it will never come to that Mr O'Reilly. Regulations will prevent that from ever being the case, we will always see any sign of a recession coming in good time to adjust lending to balance the situation!"

"I'm sorry Jones. We are wasting each others time."

Sean was exasperated with his old adversary, and turned on his heels to leave.

As he opened the office door he turned to the 'advisor' with his passing shot;

"The bubble *is* going to burst. When it does I won't say 'I told you so', and I will not lift a finger to help you when it does!"

Horton Associates would henceforth be avoided!

Victor Harvey was furious when he heard what Jones had been up to. There was a danger that his anonymity was compromised. If O'Reilly discovered his true identity his crooked world would be in jeopardy.

"Jones, I want to talk to you. Now!"

Jones knew that tone of voice and wasted no time in vacating his office and scurrying to the lift to carry him up to the penthouse suite to be humiliated once again!

"Why did you do the O'Reilly interview? After what happened the last time you screwed up I would have thought you'd have had more common sense."

"I'm more than qualified to advise him sir as you are aware. I was going to steer him towards your hedge fund!"

"It's a damn good job he realised it was you and walked away. I'll tell you this, don't *ever* contact him again. He's far too smart these days to go for anything *you* suggest. I have my own way of relieving him of his money."

"I'm sorry you think like that. I'm sure I could have persuaded him to accept my advice."

"Stop being an idiot Jones for heaven's sake!"

Victor Harvey didn't suffer fools gladly, or otherwise.

75

Liam's career took off very early in his working life when he was a young solicitor. An important client of the firm he worked for had been tricked into investing in a classic car scam.

It was quite a clever swindle perpetrated by a young member of the aristocracy.

Jeremy Truscott-Jamieson was the son of an Earl, albeit an Irish one, nevertheless a convincing con man. The idea was to test drive for the day, quality cars borrowed from main dealers whose salesmen co-operated after accepting generous bribes, then drive this car to a top London hotel where it would be 'rented out' for the day to well heeled foreign visitors at a premium. The 'hirer' invariably employed Jeremy or one of the army of drivers to drive him and guest around the sights. In itself this was a good scam, when the idea was sold as a franchise it made the fraudster a mint of crooked money! Liam represented the dealer in Bentley and Porche cars who had been swindled by Jeremy and his gang of 'borrowers' and was responsible for the prosecution of Jeremy Truscott-Jamieson successfully. It was a high profile case at the time which made Liam quite famous and popular among the influential city movers and shakers. The younger twins Michael and Jonathan lived almost parallel lives.

Michael with his fair hair and deep blue eyes, slim shape and quiet manner was attractive to the opposite sex. Whenever he was in mixed company he was surrounded by pretty girls all vying for his attention! Jonathan was equally popular but for different attributes. His hair was dark almost black, he had brown eyes with long dark lashes. A rugby player of note. Six feet four inches tall with broad shoulders and slim hips. Michael was a naturally astute businessman with a good head for figures, a talent necessary to succeed in his chosen profession, accountancy. Jonathan's temperament matched his physique, a brusque professional lawyer specialising in business law at which he was extremely successful just like his elder brother, Liam.

Now the O'Reilly family owned a powerful business empire which was to grow to make each member of it individually wealthy and famous. Sean and Rachel had enjoyed many years financial success as they raised their sons.

Much of this had been acquired by accident, one venture seemed to propel itself into another by its need. The Mick's Mix business owed its existence to the pig farm following the slurry problem. Ideas supplied by each member of staff together with a constant input from Bill Fraser, were always explored with pragmatism. Only those with definite potential would be debated until compromise indicated further research and possible action always bore fruit financially. This procedure ensured success and became the company's standard system.

The bulk of the family's fortune, which by two thousand and three was measured in tens of millions of pounds sterling was generated by the activities on the fifteen thousand pound original investment. Buying the airfield back in the sixties seemed an extravagance at the time. Of course many people were involved and many of these eventually enjoyed successful careers of their own.

At Bill's instigation the airfield was developed just in time to cash in on the new package holiday to the sunshine trade.

There was also lively private flying activity from the place, not all of which could be termed strictly legal in the activity in which the aircraft were employed. This place was the destination of flights carrying dubious characters with a reputation for nefarious business dealings. It was also the departure point for suitcases stuffed with high value bank notes destined for tax free deposit in banks on the Isle of Man.

Regulations and good practice by the government put an end to the prolific traffic, making this Island a squeaky-clean financial centre in the process.

Bill Fraser was a powerhouse of a C.E.O. of O'Reilly enterprises, his steady fiscal skill steered the cash into 'safe' investments. Bill's contacts high up the financial investments ladder included the affable John Shepherd who used the airfield extensively during his meteoric rise in banking and investment circles. John's journeys to UK and Europe for his business commitments were made possible with the use of his small twin engined Piper Navajo aircraft. As his interests spread across the Atlantic to embrace the dollar he up-graded his mode of transport to include a Lear Jet and Cessna Citation luxury private jet aircraft. Both of these machines were based and serviced at the young airport. Direct access to his interests in the U.S. was now possible.

76

Joe Kennish had an interesting day at the London Stock Exchange. The procedures for taking the distillery into the public domain were explained and understood by the assembled novices.

The broker Joe was working with, was employed by a well known firm… Horton's, and went by the name of Hugh Watson.

The two of them seemed to enjoy each other's company and worked well together preparing the company for its flotation. During these preparations it was proposed that the three shareholders should be allocated a substantial bonus and a generous block of preferential shares as part of a deal on conclusion of the flotation. Hugh Watson announced that he had some corporate clients who would be keen to obtain large shareholdings of such an attractive company. The signs were encouraging for a speedy sale of the business, freeing Sean and Rachel from their unwilling responsibility.

Paddy was happy to leave most of these preparations to the experts.

Having been totally against the idea of parting with his 'baby' for so many years it seemed sensible to hand over the responsibility and the stress involved to those mentally equipped to deal with it. This didn't mean of course that he wasn't interested in the procedure....

Good old Hugh would make sure his interests were protected.

What a wonderful friend he had become, and the concern he expressed concerning the company's future was quite extraordinary for someone who had no financial interest in it !

When he voiced this appreciation to Sean it set alarm bells ringing in Sean's head. *Why would anyone be so keen to help when they had no financial interest?* Again doubts were appearing regarding this gentleman.

Sean decided to get the lads to do some research into this Hugh Watson, Urgently!

"Liam see what you can dig up on a Mr Hugh Watson based in Dublin will you. Whilst you're at it check the companies register. I'm sure there's something fishy about him."

"OK Dad I'll start right away. I take it it's something to do with the 'pop' factory, yes?"

"Yeah , it's just a feeling at the moment, he just seems too keen to help for my liking."

Bill Fraser was also approached to see if he knew the individual. There must be any amount of information about someone as wealthy as he seems to be. After all, he's been sniffing around the place for years. Throwing cash about when there was little obvious reason to do so.

A week after the enquiries started both Liam and Bill could find no trace of this mysterious benefactor.

Sean decided a full assault by the family was called for. A board meeting was arranged, all were requested to; 'Come for dinner on Sunday, We've some important business to discuss!'

Rachel catered for Sean, her three sons plus girlfriends that day. Once again the subject of Hugh Watson, his honesty and his motives needed to be examined, this time thoroughly.

Years had passed since his integrity was first questioned but never examined. Now it was necessary to make sure he couldn't cause trouble.

Jonathan went down to Dublin the following morning, Paddy needed to be grilled about his wealthy friend directly. Trying to discover anything about Hugh Watson without Paddy's knowledge was getting them nowhere. Initially it was thought better to make discreet enquiries before getting Paddy involved, he might be reluctant to investigate his friend just because Sean didn't trust the man. Liam greeted Paddy in his usual fashion when he arrived at the distillery.

"Hi there you old rogue. What mischief have you been up to since I last saw you?" he queried. "If it isn't the snotty nosed young Jonny boy then." Came the affectionate reply.

"I suppose you want some of the 'special' do yer? Sean should come down and fetch his own!"

"To be sure I'll be wanting to take a drop or two back with me when I leave."

"So Jonny, what's the real reason for your visit?

"We're getting near the big sell off Paddy and we are all wondering about this rich pal of yours. What's his name, Hugh Wilson?"

"Watson , Hugh Watson. Why?

"He seems very interested in getting involved in the flotation that's all.

Perhaps a little too interested. Any idea why?"

Paddy scratched his head as though searching for an answer.

"Hell no, he's always been interested, ever since we first met him. Is there any reason why he shouldn't be Jonathan?"

"I really don't know Paddy, that's the problem. None of us up there can think of any reason other than he wants to get his hands on the hooch. You don't get as rich as he seems to be by being just a good friend. We feel there has to be a financial motive."

"He has never tried to suggest we sell him any of the action. Nor has he ever wanted us to 'go public' with the business."

"Well can you think of anything, has he asked for the recipe or any figures for sales, profits that sort of thing?"

"No. Not that I can remember, certainly not recently."

"What do you mean Paddy, not recently?"

"Well he did ask us how we made the stuff so powerful, compared to everyone else's."

"Did either of you tell him. Give him a clue?"

"No Jonathan, absolutely not. I didn't and I'm certain Nellie didn't. The secret is and always has been, sacrosanct. The whole value of the product depends on never disclosing the reason for the liquor strength."

"I understand that. I have to conclude that your Mr Watson is up to no good as far as our company is concerned. Be on your guard whatever you do Paddy.

I'm sure he'll make a move soon. Let us know when he does won't you?"

77

Sean and Rachel thought it was about time their sons were now directly involved with the 'empire'. They had established fine careers of their own of course, but the O'Reilly brand was their inheritance and they needed to understand everything about it.

There were so many divisions now. The airport was a bustling meeting place for the airlines and their clients. What was once an almost derelict aerodrome now had two terminals. One to cater for relatively local flights, those within the United Kingdom and the new large terminal for long haul and package holiday flights. This was now one of the most modern airports in Europe, and one of the busiest. Other interests included business aircraft charter, servicing and repairing machines.

Away from the flying activities were the insurance and mortgage companies, car hire and taxi firms, scrap metal dealership and recycling plant. All of which were leaders in their field and all producing enormous wealth for the O'Reilly group.

As the family's chartered accountant it was decided that Michael should take over the financial sectors which Bill had been responsible for since he joined the company.

Sean had difficulty in persuading Bill to retire, his energy seemed boundless even though he was now well into his seventies. In the end it was Jane who was able to persuade him to step down on the understanding that they would buy a home in sunnier climes. Spain beckoned.

Michael decided to scrutinise the accounts of each of his new responsibilities and put his own mark on them. He announced his intention to the heads of each department. It came as a surprise to him and the rest of the family when there was a mad exodus by these top level executives before he had even started!

Alarm bells started ringing with a deafening urgency. Why on earth should these very well paid people jump ship in such a hurry? The answer appeared almost as soon as the first balance sheet was presented to Michael by one of the filing clerks.

There was obviously criminal activity going on. This first glance at the books of the airport showed very different figures to the ones that had been presented at Bill's year's end report. The bottom line of these figures was many thousands of pounds less than the actual figures suggested which meant that huge sums had been creamed off by someone. The same result occurred at each of the main enterprises. It was pretty obvious that far too much trust had been placed in the managers. Sean had never checked up personally. That was Bill's job! Michael tried to contact Bill to try and find out what had been going on behind his father's back!

There was a small problem now, Bill could not be found. His house was deserted. Sean was shattered. This man had been trusted for so many years, even treated almost as a brother. Why did he do this?. How *could* he do it? As Michael went painstakingly through every scrap of paper, every file on every computer he found evidence of fraud on a gigantic scale.

This would have to be turned over to the Serious Fraud squad of the Police, but not quite yet! Sean tried to trace his ex best friend through the airline which must have carried him and Jane to their retirement destination. At first he thought it should be an easy matter to trace them. It was Spain he said he was retiring to wasn't it?

Obviously many years practice of deceit had taught him to lie about anything and everything. He wouldn't have gone anywhere near Spain now would he? Sean decided to try and find out more from Bill's old superior, John Shepherd and contacted him by phone.

"Mr Shepherd? Sean O'Reilly here. I wonder if you can help me. I'm looking for Bill Fraser, you wouldn't know where I might find him would you?"

"I'm sorry Mr O'Reilly, I haven't seen him for some time. May I be of some help otherwise?"

"I just need to talk to him soon that's all." Sean was surprised at Shepherd's reaction as they were supposed to be in touch on an almost daily basis it seemed virtually impossible that he hadn't been in contact for some time. Very curious......

7 8

Paddy had done all he could to see that the distillery was in top condition prior to the public getting visual access to the plant before purchasing shares at the flotation. There was only a week to go before the 'Big Day'. A series of open house sessions had seen a procession of city suited businessmen asking endless questions about the company's performance and projected profit. Paddy enjoyed telling them all about the outstanding success they had enjoyed since the company was formed. Hugh Watson was a little agitated when he saw the state of the liquor holding tank. It looked absolutely disgusting! There was rust around the discharge valve and a pool of grey sludge around its base.

"Paddy old chap, I think we'd better get rid of that dirty tank.

I know where we could get a brand new stainless one today and have it working in time for the floatation." Paddy was about to say that would probably be the biggest mistake possible but checked himself. What a brilliant idea he thought. Once they'd picked up their cheques and shares it would no longer matter what the stuff was like! The contents of the old tank were put in the system for processing. This would be the last decent blend to be produced, after this the quality would drop to be a very ordinary, average quality potcheen which would probably be difficult to sell. Ah well, the new lovely shiny tanks really did improve the appearance of the place. Very posh indeed!

The flotation was a success, all shares were pre-sold at the prescribed price. The company was no longer any part of the O'Reilly's lives. Sean was pleased. He sold his preference shares to John Shepherd for their face value. A large bouquet of flowers was delivered to Rachel the following day. The note with the blooms said; 'To dear Rachel with kindest regards, John'. There was also a bottle of twelve year old single malt Scotch Whisky also accompanied by a card with the words; 'Sean, thanks for everything. John.' Both notes were hand written in very artistic copper plate!

79

The American economy was in total melt-down. Banks were crashing on a daily basis. The two biggest mortgage companies had to be rescued by the US treasury, closely followed by enormous injections of capital into all the banks. The reason for this collapse was the totally incompetent lending by those institutions. Phrases such as 'Toxic debt' and 'Global recession' were bandied about by the governments and media.

In tandem with the American failures, the United Kingdom showed the same levels of criminal incompetence by the banks and building societies. These failures were exacerbated by knee-jerk government action pouring oceans of cash into the banks' self -made 'black holes'. In effect the banks had made themselves bankrupt by lending too much money to house buyers and companies who simply didn't earn enough to be able to withstand any disruption to their lives. The O'Reillys suffered as everyone else did. Huge losses occurred as business contracted. Sean and Rachel felt responsible for all the employees at their various companies. Sean understood the reasons for the calamity, he had been warning government agents for ten years that regulations were too weak and the bonus culture was responsible for the majority of the failure. It was always his company policy to pay senior management fairly with any bonus to be shared by *all* the employees as they were the ones responsible for any success. This was greatly appreciated by the workforce. The successful results of his companies bore witness to the good sense and loyalty shown by both sides.

The month following the flotation of the Kilmona Distillery the shares gained in value rapidly. The new management had an excellent advertising company who were really on the ball with their TV advertising. Clever stuff , which grabbed the attention of the public. Sales were breaking all records.

Hugh Fraser was pleased with his new acquisition. Having obtained over seventy per cent of the general shares together with all the preference shares. It had cost him an absolute fortune. He'd had to sell most of his other investments in order to get to this position. Still, it was obviously worth it. People were always going to drink Irish Whiskey and his was known to be the best. Paddy felt a little guilty at allowing his generous friend to be in this position. Once that last brew was sold, which wouldn't take long at the rate the stuff was leaving the premises, the complaints would take a bit of shine off the sales! Paddy told Sean what had happened during the disposal of all their shares and who had jumped at the chance to snap them all up at the inflated price of the preferential ones.

"Well Paddy, I haven't found out who he is yet, but the boys are working on it. Something is just not right about him……

8 ⊘

Jonathon and Michael were examining every corner of the business with a thoroughness only those involved in a family concern would be prepared to do. The name John Shepherd kept appearing where large purchases were made. All this information was coming out during a search of Bill Watson's private records. When Sean was given the information he was absolutely shocked. He considered himself a good judge of character. John Shepherd, like Bill had appeared to be such a good friend. So much of the family fortune had been made because of his advice. Liam was going to have to investigate this man. Rachel was very upset that her good friend Jane Watson had vanished with her husband. How could she behave as an apparently close friend knowing what Bill was up to? Thinking about this she was convinced that Jane didn't know. She couldn't have had a clue.

Sean was wondering how the conspiracy could have remained such a close secret between Bill and John Shepherd. Thinking of John Shepherd made him remember the card with the Whisky. That writing, he was sure he'd seen some other note with similar writing. When was it? Where was it? A quick search in his desk revealed the note he had been given by Paddy which was advising him not to float the booze business. The writing was identical! Michael discovered serious fraudulent expenditure on exorbitant 'bonus' payments to several of the senior managers. These payments were paid regardless of company performance.

The worst excesses involved the mortgage company, the hire purchase company and the brokerage firm. In fact all the O'Reilly finance departments.

Michael also discovered the purchase by the company of a Lear Jet and Cessna Citation. The paper-work for these had been signed ostensibly by Sean! It was now obvious that the scale of criminal activity demanded the attention of the police. Certainly as far as Bill Fraser was concerned. This character needed to be found. Urgently. Heaven knows how much worse the damage was going to be. The bank statements from the various companies showed that the day before Bill disappeared all fluid cash had been withdrawn. To all intents and purposes the family was temporarily insolvent. Two senior officers from the serious fraud squad started their investigations almost at once. Sean was the first witness to be questioned.

"How much of this activity were you aware of Mr O'Reilly?"

"Absolutely none of it Inspector. If I had any idea of dishonesty I wouldn't be talking to you now. Unfortunately things have gone much too far for me to deal with any of it myself."

"Have you any idea where Mr Fraser may have gone?"

"No I haven't, he never mentioned any other family or where he came from.

Right from the first time we met we trusted him completely. Believe me he was a very plausible character. Rachel is convinced that his wife Jane has no idea what he's been up to. I wouldn't know where to start, unless…."

"Unless what Mr O'Reilly?"

"Unless he's in contact with John Shepherd. He's the other banker I mentioned. Another man we trusted completely…. Until now."

"You think he may be part of a conspiracy, this Shepherd chap?"

"Nothing certain. Just a feeling I have that he may be"

"What do you mean by that?"

"Well there are a couple of hand written notes which are supposed to have been written by two different people, sent to me.

One of them was written some time ago the other only recently but they look suspiciously similar to me."

"May I see them ?"

"Of course. Just give me five minutes to find them."

When the detective saw the notes Sean had received from John Shepherd and Hugh Watson he was of the same opinion.

"I'd better keep these and get them checked out by one of our experts. Do you mind?"

"Of course not."

"This letter suggests he was involved with another company. Is it one of your companies?"

"Only that my wife and I had a financial interest through her mother. It was her mother's firm down in Dublin. You may have heard of it 'Kilmona Whiskey'?"

"Oh yes, my favourite tipple. Better than Scotch in my opinion!"

Sean explained briefly, the history.

"Thanks for your help, I will let you know if we find Fraser.

"In the meantime if you find out any more, please let us know."

It was no surprise to discover another fan of the liquid treasure that was Kilmona Potcheen. Another friend to help solve the identity of the mystery man who had been involved in their lives for years maintaining his anonymity and motives!

81

The last of the 'special' was quickly disposed of and the new brew was a poor replacement for the Nellie and Paddy original. The alcohol had been found wanting, the flavour bland and ordinary. Certainly this wasn't going to set the world on fire like its predecessor! Sean heard from Paddy that his good friend Hugh wasn't at all pleased, his investment was threatened with a severe clout if things didn't improve and very quickly. "Are you in touch with him at the moment Paddy? The police this end are pretty sure he's up to his neck in criminal activity. If so it would explain his generosity to you and Nell".

It didn't make any sense. Why would someone like him take so long about it if he was attempting to con them. Particularly as he had tried to stop them going public? He could have easily persuaded them to follow Sean's advice ages ago and gained control at a much better price.

Paddy tried hard to understand the reasoning of his friend. All the advice he'd given them had seemed to be in their interest.

It eventually dawned on him that Nelly and his own reluctance to explain how the difference in the alcohol content was obtained. He had been obviously been trying to find out in order to use the formula with a rival distillery which he would have been able to buy for a fraction of the price of Kilmona PLC. Some friend.

82

The financial melt-down in the US banks and financial markets was affecting financial centres world-wide. The cause of the disaster was incompetent practice by all these 'money lending' agencies. They had accumulated massive losses by lending too much cash to too many people for houses they could not afford to purchase. These 'Toxic' holdings were simply enormous. The market for property had been driven by the practice of lending cheaply no questions asked. Sean was not very surprised when the crash came. His own policy had always erred on the side of safety, the mortgages he offered were on the basis of ninety percent of the purchase price of the property at a fixed rate of interest which was always less than the banks demanded. The value of properties considered was capped at one hundred and fifty thousand pounds. The property had to be new build also.

Providing the prospective client could prove his or her income was sufficient to enable easy affordability, the mortgage was usually granted. No one had reneged in the last ten years.

In contrast, the big banks and building societies had only been interested in providing obscene un-earned bonuses for the executives. It was this difference which saved the O'Reilly group from a similar disastrous failure.

83

Only a few months after the distillery had 'gone public' sales had simply crashed. Shareholders had quickly realised that they had bought into a total flop. They disposed of most of their shares cheaply in an uncomfortable haste. Too quickly for Hugh to rid himself of his own shares at a price which was not ruinous. In fact the initial price of two pounds fifty per share was now worth only two pence! Paddy was not born yesterday he knew precisely why the shares had dived he also knew how to make them rise again. Using a tiny fraction of the cash he had received when he sold his preferential shares he bought into Kilmona Whiskey blocks of shares, sparingly. He only bought when they were valued at under ten pence. It only took six weeks to buy up most of the shares which Hugh didn't own. Paddy's old friend had changed his spots dramatically! " What did you do to the stuff you swine?"

"I don't know what you're talking about Hugh. What do you mean?"

"The whiskey is awful. No-one wants it. You must have changed the formula . Did you?"

"Of course not, it's probably this ruddy credit crunch of yours."

"My credit crunch, *my* credit crunch?" He was shouting now.

"Yes Hugh. *Your* credit crunch! You *are* a senior banker aren't you?"

Hugh Watson was not a happy man. A good deal of his fortune has been lost with this disastrous venture. Paddy saw an opportunity to buy the remaining shares for a song. The offer he was going to make had to be done now whist Hugh was down in the depths of depression. He had to feel sorry for the man, it was so obvious to Paddy that this 'friend' had been using Nellie and himself to get control of the gold-mine that the distillery had been. Serves him right. "I wish I'd never met you and Nellie. I'm ruined you know!"

"Look Hugh. I'm very sorry about what's happened. What are you going to do now?"

"I don't have a clue. Go back to banking I suppose. One thing's for sure I'm getting rid of the damn shares as soon as I can find a mug to buy them!

"If it'll help I'll shift them for you if you like?"

"If you can find a buyer quickly I'll give you ten per cent in cash!"

"OK Give me a couple of days." Paddy rang Sean as soon as Hugh Watson switched off his mobile phone.

"Sean I've just had Hugh Watson on the phone. He's been crying into his potcheen! Would you believe the Kilmona brand is no longer the 'must have' bottle on the connoisseur's table?

Without the 'special' ingredient the firm has crashed and he wants to dump his interest. I've offered to find a buyer for his shares."

"Right I need to talk to that gentleman, I'm pretty certain he's a crook. Make an appointment to meet him again. Tell him you've found a buyer for him, then call me back Paddy. This is very important." Sean immediately contacted the officer from the fraud squad.

Detective Inspector Davis was quick to appreciate the opportunity which was now developing. If Mr Watson was the same person as Mr Shepherd as Sean suspected, the inquiry should soon provide results. It all depended on a face to face meeting. If they were one and the same person the connection would be established between John Shepherd and Bill Fraser.

"I'll send a couple of officers down to Dublin to talk to the Garda. We'll need their co-operation to be able to arrest him. We'll have to get this op. organised as soon as possible. If he is involved with Fraser I don't want him doing a runner."

Paddy was briefed to organise a meeting with Hugh Fraser for the following Monday. This would allow time over the weekend to liase with the officers from the Dublin police.

"Yes Hugh, that's right. Monday next. How about ten o'clock at the distillery?"

"Have you found a buyer for me?"

"If the price is right I'm pretty sure so, yes. By the way what is your price?"

"I'll accept whatever you can get. You won't swindle me will you?"

"Of course not Hugh!"

The police investigation at the airport was carried out in a thoroughly professional manner. After a week searching the offices the employees were interviewed, Bill Fraser's secretary experienced the hardest week of her life.

There was little she could tell the police which would move the investigation forward. Bill would only allow her in his office when he needed her to take dictation for sending a letter or witnessing document signing.

"Didn't you think this a strange way for your boss to behave?" asked the female sergeant who was trying to discover how the fraud was able to continue so successfully for so long.

"Not really no. Mr Fraser was always very polite, very pleasant."

"What about clients who visited him? Were you present at any meetings he had with them?"

"He only ever had one visitor that I can remember during my time as his secretary."

"This visitor, was it a man or a woman?"

"A man. Mr Shepherd. I was always sent on some errand when he was here."

"These errands. Were they ones which would seem normal to you at the time?"

"Yes. They were usually to do with one or other of Mr Shepherd's aircraft. Either the Citation or the Lear Jet" The sergeant turned to Michael at this point to enquire as to the legal ownership of the aircraft concerned. Michael was able to confirm that these machines were purchased using O' Reilly cash.

"Our good friend Mr Shepherd has been taking us for a wee jaunt lads.

We'll need to find a way of getting his bank to reimburse us." exclaimed Sean.

"I think a substantial jail term for the two of them must be expected. Always provided we can find them of course."

"I think dad has his own plans for this man" Michael said. The fraud squad team were now on the trail of two experienced con artists. It was obvious that the two had made an art of conspiracy. The O'Reillys were no fools themselves.

Retribution would follow without vengeance.

When the results of the handwriting specialist confirmed that John Shepherd and Hugh Watson were one and the same, the investigation changed up a couple of gears.

The first port of call for the detective handling the initial moves was the head office of the bank where the two were employed.

An appointment to interview the managing director was made.

"Can you give me the address of your fellow director John Shepherd?" was the opening question to Mr Roland Morgan the Chief Executive of the bank.

"No officer I'm afraid I can't."

"Can't sir, or won't?"

"Can't. We don't have a Mr Shepherd working for this bank."

"When did he resign?"

"Like I said, we don't have a Shepherd on our staff, Never have had."

The officers were not really surprised at this revelation. Their suspicions were now confirmed. The next step was to liase with the Garda in Dublin. Hugh Watson was the next suspect on their list.

Rachel was concerned about Sean, recent events were causing a great deal of anxiety for him. To have been so wrong about Bill Fraser. To have put so much trust in him and to have worked with him all these years without getting any idea of the conspiracy left him feeling totally inadequate. For the first time in his life he felt uncontrollably angry. An anger which was burning into his soul,

it made him feel very uncomfortable. Whilst she too felt anger Rachel did her best to understand how he felt.

"He took everyone in Sean. Me, Sheila, Paddy, Mickey even Nelly liked and trusted him. You must try not to reproach yourself. The only thing to do now is to find him and make sure he pays for his treacherous behaviour."

"I will Rachel, oh I will! and when I do I want him to feel as angry we are right now."

"What do you mean Sean?"

"I want to take everything he owns. Every penny of the money he's had from us. Totally destroy him together with that parasite Shepherd or whatever his real name is."

"Be careful darling they are probably very dangerous."

84

The distillery was quiet when Paddy arrived, he wanted to make sure there was a good vantage point for the detectives and Sean when Watson arrived. It was almost nine o'clock when Sean and the police arrived . The Garda were waiting for them at the main gate to the premises so that they could all go inside together.

There was a small office off the entrance lobby which allowed space for the group to assemble unseen from anyone entering the building. At exactly ten o'clock there was the sound of a car door closing followed by footsteps on the paving outside.

The group waited in total silence as the visitor opened the door and strode into the building towards the waiting figure of Paddy McCormick. Instead of the impressive figure expected, a diminutive frame approached with his arm outstretched offering his hand for shaking.

"Hello Mr McCormick, my name is Jones, Derek Jones . How do you do?"

"Where is Mr Watson, hasn't he come with you?"

"He is indisposed unfortunately. He asked me to bring some shares to you. I understand you have some cash for him?"

It was agreed with the police that the transaction should take place before Mr Watson was apprehended. With the organ grinder absent it was decided to interview his monkey instead!

8 5

Philip Baverstock was in conference with fellow directors of the bank on Grand Cayman Island. A crisis was looming in the boardroom.

American financial houses were indicating a melt-down in their mortgage world. The two biggest mortgage lenders had virtually bankrupted themselves after ten years of un-realistic lending. The lending policy had been designed to force up the value of houses by making unlimited cash available to anyone and everyone. The net result of this incomprehensible nonsense was a total collapse of the housing market. All the American financial institutions had been borrowing money from banks across the continent who in turn were drawing loans from banks across the globe. A recipe for disaster.

"I understand most of them will be approaching their government for assistance." Philip Baverstock replied to a concerned colleague.

"Don't worry about it. The whole thing is such a mess that the blame will be a collective one. We're fireproof!!"

"But we are responsible for taking the risks. We are the policy makers. Surely the government will recognise this?" another executive suggested.

"What we *must* do is make sure we get our bonus payments sorted as soon as possible!"

The extent of Philip Baverstock's arrogance took their breath away. Some of the gathering even felt a small degree of guilt for the chaos they had collectively caused!

86

Paddy ushered Derek Jones into the boardroom where he was confronted by the gathering of police and at the front of the group stood Sean O'Reilly.

"Where's your boss Jones. Why do I *always* have to make do with you?"

Jones raised both his arms in supplication at the unfriendly verbal assault.

"You deserve an explanation Mr O'Reilly, I really do understand how you must feel. All you've ever had from me over these years seems to have been totally unhelpful!"

"That has to be the understatement of the century!"

Sean stated in reply.

"I really was trying to protect you and your lovely wife."

"I'm looking forward to listening to your reasoning Jones. If it hadn't been for the intervention by Bill Fraser and John Shepherd we would not be here talking about it!"

"Quite so Mr O'Reilly. Your *friends* Fraser and Shepherd saw you both as the couple of farming losers! I did my best to protect you by denying those loans you wanted. It was made very clear to me that my job and my home would be 'taken away' if I didn't co-operate with them. Shepherd knew that the aerodrome was going to be sold by the British government and according to normal policy offered to the sitting tenant. You."

Sean was astonished. It was all beginning to make sense. No wonder the two of them were so friendly, they wanted the airfield for their own criminal activities. There was a bonus in it after they had control, O'Reilly cash. The building of the terminal, the two private jet aircraft. God knows what else they're up to!"

It looks like Rachel and I may have got you wrong Mr Jones."

"Would you mind addressing me as Derek, Mr O'Reilly?"

Sean laughed when he heard this, what a ludicrous situation. All these years he had hated this little man. Treated him with total contempt. Right now it looks as though finally, Mr Jones will be able to help him and Rachel.

"OK Derek if you insist, and you may as well call me Sean." They shook hands for the very first time!

"I really would like to help if I can, to deal with Fraser and Shepherd if that's your intention?"

"Thanks Derek I'm sure you will be an enormous help. You must have a good idea what the pair of them have been up to over the years"

"Where do you want me to start? "

"Let's try the beginning shall we? Anything unusual or dishonest they did either together or individually. And not necessarily concerning Rachel or me."

87

Paddy now owned the majority of the shares in Kilmona Whiskey.

Having legally purchased the largest block from Shepherd he could now set about restoring the galvanised storage tank! It was obviously going to take some time to restore the reputation of the product but at least Paddy knew that the stuff would soon be in demand again. A substantial programme of promotion was called for. Free samples to his old clients would be the start of this process.

It was such a strange business when his old friend Hugh sent his underling to finalise the deal they had. Still, no matter...

It was now obvious that Hugh wanted to keep out of sight. Perhaps he had realised that Paddy had worked out what he had been up to. No matter. Kilmona whisky was back in his hands. Maybe he'd just keep his shares and employ someone to run the company. There again maybe he wouldn't!

88

Philip Baverstock was in the Isle of Man. The purpose of this visit was to transfer a couple of million dollars into one of his American companies. The particular business was a 'respectable' mortgage company, in reality it was used to launder funds gained from illegal activity in Europe. A substantial amount had been generated at an ex RAF airfield in Northern Ireland. This cash was going to be transferred into an account in his real name, Victor Harvey. So far he had no idea that his colleague Bill Fraser, had evacuated his position as head of their mutual illegal 'gold mine'.

All was very satisfactory as far as he knew. This latest movement of cash would arrive from the Isle of Man overnight, in the morning it would be ready to move again, or so he thought.

Michael in going through the items he found on the computer in Fraser's office noticed a sum of two hundred and ten thousand pounds was due to be sent from the company pension account to an investment company in the Cayman Islands called 'Baverstock Holdings'. Michael had not heard of the company so he rang Joe Kennish, Sean and Rachel's personal accountant.

"Hi Joe, have you ever heard of a company called Baverstock based in the Caymans?"

"Yes. It's one of the investment companies that your Dad has been using for the company pension fund. It was included in a bunch of off shore banks recommended by John Shepherd some years ago."

The trail began…..

Sean reflected on his mistake in trusting his 'friend' totally. The behaviour of Derek Jones at the bank had given the two crooks the opportunity to operate their colossal fraud.

Rachel had been right, there was no use wasting time on self recrimination, this would be better spent working out ways of recovering their money. Whilst these two had been operating, Sean had been heavily involved in his council obligations which was a full time job. Only occasionally was he in the company office, usually to assist one of his constituents with purchasing a home or small business premises. Without his help few of them would have been successful.

Derek Jones was now assisting the O'Reilly brothers in unravelling the tangle of crooked business deals perpetrated by Fraser and Shepherd. It was now known that 'Shepherd' was using at least one alias. Derek Jones was able to confirm the connection with the distillery and its 'best friend' Hugh Watson.

"How did you become under so much control from these two Derek?" Jonathan asked. A visibly embarrassed Derek Jones spluttered

"I borrowed money from the bank's pension fund to put down on my home. I know it was stupid and realise it was a criminal act, but I did intend to repay the money quickly. Unfortunately Mr Fraser did a spot check before I was able to return all of it. The next day Mr Shepherd arrived at my branch and told me I was going to be prosecuted and would undoubtedly go to prison as well as losing my home, I was terrified. If all that happened I would have lost my wife as well."

"So that was when he blackmailed you was it? " Michael asked.

"Oh No, that came much later. I was kept waiting, wondering, worrying for weeks....months. Eventually your father came on the scene. Mr Fraser came into the office and told me to deny any help to him, your father. I wasn't told why I was to do it. I only knew by the way that he said it that it wasn't a choice that I had."

"Did you have any idea at that time what his motive was."

"Not a clue, I thought it a most unfair way to treat the man who seemed very pleasant. "

"Had you managed to replace the money by this time?"

"Yes, I realised that if I could get it back before I was arrested the court might be a little lenient and not put me in prison."

"So the pair of them no longer had a real hold over you did they?"

"Theoretically no they didn't but they were my bosses and were always going to be in a position to sack me without a reference. That was made very clear by the director Shepherd."

Jonathan grilled him for over an hour at the end of which both he and Michael were convinced he was telling the truth and had no direct part in the scam.

"Right Derek. How do you fancy helping us catch the pair of them?"

Derek Jones' eyes lit up at the invitation for him to assist in putting things right, retribution would be so sweet! They had to establish exactly who Shepherd and Watson were. Derek Jones had access to head office personnel. His first job was to go back to his office and find out.

Michael and Jonathan discussed the days happenings at dinner with Sean, Rachel and Liam. Liam had spent the day searching for information on Bill Fraser and John Shepherd.

Interestingly it wasn't too difficult with Fraser, he had been investigated about mortgage irregularities but nothing positive was proven. He had been very fortunate at his chosen profession. A natural talent for all things banking. He was used extensively by the directors of the banks he worked for, all sorts of borderline deals. Bill Fraser was at the forefront of the scandalous policy of lending by the bank for building at any cost. To Fraser and Shepherd the only goal worth chasing was money and any risk was worth taking to achieve each dubious success. Sean and Rachel seemed the perfect candidates for a major boost to the criminal pair's pension funds.

If they could be enticed into purchasing the airport for them their 'import and export' business would flourish! In control of that place there was no end to opportunities which would present themselves. Easy, so easy to shift suitcases of cash by private aircraft to the Isle of Man, which Shepherd did for years until the Isle of Man government put its fiscal house in order. This sensible action by the Manx government increased its usefulness as a home for the O'Reilly legitimate pension fund investments. Using careful management through dealings with the Baverstock bank in the US.

89

Paddy McCormick was in his element now. The Kilmona Whisky company was now back in the best hands. Following the successful acquisition of all those shares. The 'new brew' was very quickly produced. A new logo featuring a large pig with its title 'Big Boar Brew' in gold letters inscribed around the pig design was a cheeky stab at Hugh Watson. The greedy pig!

Paddy had learned a trick or two about marketing since meeting Nellie Flanagan. The promotion he put together on television across all channels for a month when the first of the 'triple B' was ready was stunningly effective, featuring a cartoon of a boar which bore a remarkable resemblance to Watson! The most important part of the sales pitch was to send a crate of this excellent stuff to each of the royal households in Britain; Buckingham Palace, Windsor Castle, Balmoral, Sandringham, Clarence House and Kensington Palace. The embassies were not forgotten either. Every military headquarters received the same generous gesture. All this was done through its registered office at the airport business centre, which was of course on UK territory. The thinking behind this came from Paddy's desire to obtain the coveted Royal Warrant. It was a recognised fact that this warrant guaranteed success in retailing and so it was that the invitation came to regularly supply Her Majesty with the very acceptable product. This was quickly followed with a large order from both houses of parliament.

9 ∅

Derek Jones went back to his office with a spring in his step and a determined countenance which was quickly noticed by the staff. One by one the office juniors were summoned into his office and quizzed carefully. The 'true' identity of Shepherd-Watson was discovered by accident. A junior cleaner had been responsible for emptying the wastepaper basket in Shepherd's office.

Among the papers she removed were several official looking envelopes with important sender's post marks. Some of these had the government portcullis stamp. The addressee was Sir Philip Baverstock. Now they were looking for a Knight of the Realm,or so they thought.

Liam was trying to find out the extent of the conspiracy. The airport seemed to be the hub of their activities. Movement records showed that the two private jet aircraft which had been purchased with O'Reilly money had been used on a monthly basis to travel to Ronaldsway airport on the Isle of Man. The object of these trips was to be investigated as a matter of urgency. Why the Isle of Man? As far as anyone in Ireland knew there were no business connections there.

Jonathan decided to make a start over there as soon as he could get a scheduled flight. There was no justification in his mind for using the company jets for so short a flight, besides there was an injunction placed on these two machines. They were to be impounded and examined by the police forensic team. They were also getting very interested in 'Mr Shepherd' or whoever he was.

The flight to the Cayman Islands in the private jet was as usual, a pleasant interlude which gave Sir Philip time to relax. The next few days would be pretty hectic. When he left the aircraft after they landed at Grand Cayman airport he was very surprised when an airport police car pulled up as he stepped down onto the tarmac. He assumed it was sent to pick him up as the VIP he considered himself to be, and take him to his villa. A nice touch he thought.

Two officers got out of the car, one of them walked up to the front of the Citation and stuck a notice on the windscreen which effectively grounded the aircraft. Liam had set the machinery in motion to recover his company's property.

Sir Philip Baverstock was stunned. He protested with the officers who had acted to impound the aircraft.

"On who's authority are you acting officers? I don't owe any landing fees for my aircraft. I have an annual account with your airport authority."

"I'm sorry sir, there has been an instruction to impound the machine from the British CAA. Apparently there is some confusion over the ownership."

"That is *my* aircraft. I can show you the necessary documents!"

"Like I said sir, the order is from the CAA in London. We have to comply. Sorry."

The reality of what had occurred meant Philip Baverstock needed to move quickly, he dialled Bill Fraser's office phone number. When the phone rang Michael picked up the receiver.

"Who's that?" the voice demanded. Michael said nothing, waiting for the voice to continue. It didn't. The phone reverted to a dialling tone. The next call Baverstock made was to Bill's mobile phone. This time when the connection was made the two were able to converse.

"What's going on Bill? The Citation has been impounded... by the CAA apparently."

"*What*. Already? I'm sorry Philip, I was waiting for a hint of what was happening at the airport before calling you to give you the gen. on the O'Reilly investigation. I didn't think they would discover anything yet."

"What are you talking about. What investigation?"

"The pig farmers have ganged up together and it looks as though they have found out about the funds used to buy the aircraft."

"What about the rest? How much do you think they know?"

"They have their own accountant checking the files, young Mike is no fool either. I think we may have a little problem."

The internet connection between the fraud squad in Northern Ireland and its counterpart in Virginia was constantly busy now looking for any contact between the crooked protagonists.

91

The world's banks were creaking with the load of Toxic debt they had accumulated over the past nine years. This was increasingly becoming apparent as financial institutions, particularly in America and Great Britain, started falling apart with colossal debt mountains. One after another these mighty companies went cap in hand to their governments for fiscal aid to avoid total collapse. Nationalisation in fact if not in word was now inevitable including Baverstock Inc. Sir Philip had known for some time that his company's books didn't balance. He also knew because of his other banking connections, that all the other banks including those in the Far East were also suffering from the same terminal stupidity. Safety in numbers was the watch-word throughout the banking industry. So long as the bubble didn't burst on their shift it didn't matter one little jot! The present problem was that this darned bubble has gone bang and there was no way any of them could dodge out of the way. Avoiding blame was going to be a difficult challenge. The leaders of the biggest organisations were in the front line of attack from the obvious source .... the National Governments, who naturally denied any part of the calamity. 'Tighten up the regulations they all shouted, when of course they should have done just that years earlier. The signs for this disaster had been clear for months before the situation became headline news around the world. Blame was one thing, sorting out the mess was going to be quite another. In the US trillions of dollars were handed out to these incompetent institutions as a quick fix solution!

Sir Philip would join the queue of greedy bankers going to their governments with gold lined begging bowls. Just like all the others he would be given more millions of dollars in America and more millions of pounds from Britain. The fact that the British government was going to nationalise his outfit would be of little concern, he would walk away smiling with sacks of cash. Brilliant!!

When Sean found out about this possibility he was determined to bring him to justice. Somehow this crook would not be allowed to prosper in this shameful way, but if retribution was going to be effective it would have to be swift and controlled…. by the O'Reillys! Which would mean keeping him out of the hands of the police. The first move was to find a way of removing him from all the boards of banks he was presently occupying. That way only the banks would benefit from the hand-outs. Not this greedy individual. The next action would be to successfully punish him for the thieving he had done at the airport. If Sean could do that it would inevitably start the chain reaction which would bring him down. The O'Reilly family would be a powerful army of investigators to bring about the disgrace and penury Sir Philip Baverstock deserved. Each family member was given an area of investigation to cover very thoroughly. Not a clue must be missed. Michael was to continue sifting through the material in the offices at the airport, paying particular attention to any transaction which involved collaboration between Bill Fraser and 'John Shepherd'. Because of his involvement with the pair, Derek Jones was assisting as and when required. It soon became obvious that half the profitable income of the

O'Reilly company was being diverted to one 'pension fund' or another.

Putting a brake on any outward movement of these monies would 'stop the rot' dead in its tracks. There would be no more leaching towards the well-being of those two *friends*!

Liam was investigating through official records any actions that had gone through the courts against either of the protagonists. There was plenty of evidence of these, however in each case they were settled out of court. The charges ranged from demands for 'interest on debts' to physical injury caused by violence. In these actions the culprits were named. Liam discovered William Fraser's name kept cropping up. Only twice was Philip Baverstock's. His name accompanied the most violent of the charges involving serious injury and hospitalisation of the plaintiff, obviously threats or bribery caused the cases to be withdrawn. These men must be brought to justice and when they are there will be no 'charges withdrawn' for any reason whatsoever.

Jonathan's task was to be Sir Philip's 'shadow', wherever he goes and whatever he does. There was to be no hiding place.

Now was the time to start using the Lear Jet. Liam arranged with the CAA for the lifting of the injunction on the Cessna so that a couple of spare pilots could accompany him to the Owen Roberts International airport on Grand Cayman. Their job will be to fly both these aircraft back to the UK. Liam wasn't alone on the Lear Jet. With the possibility of a violent, angry confrontation with Philip Baverstock, it made sense to take precautions, and a weapon with him.

The Cayman authorities were informed that a meeting was requested with their police department. Initially, all was going to be done strictly within the law. If this approach proved unsuccessful, other action of a clandestine nature would follow.

Following the loss of his private transport, Sir Philip became somewhat agitated. What if they had discovered his true identity?

If they had, it wouldn't be long before they found out a great deal more. Time to try to cover his tracks. Bill Fraser was the first contact he made.

"Any news Bill? I haven't been able to get near the airport so far. The place is buzzing with police and O'Reilly family, I did see the Lear Jet go over earlier. I suspect that means they have started trying to find out where we are."

"I'm going into the bank this morning to get that transfer of cash done before they can stop it. After that we'd better disappear. You might as well move on straight away Bill, get a head start."

The Baverstock bank's president strode into the office looking as though he hadn't a care in the world. This was typical of his behaviour. He naturally commanded respect from all his employees. He went straight to his computer, fired it up and prepared to divest the O'Reilly pension fund of another chunk of its wealth. After he logged on, the screen quickly informed him he was too late.

'Account Frozen' appeared in strong letters.

"Damn." he muttered. His personal secretary queried this exclamation.

"Is there anything wrong sir? Anything I can do to help?"

"No Janet, just a small problem. How are things here? regarding the so called 'Credit Crunch'. Anyone from the government visited us yet?"

"No sir, but I have made an appointment for you to see the minister tomorrow."

"Here?"

"No. At the Treasury, ten fifteen. The chief himself wants to talk with you." All was not well with the Cayman financial sector. Funds were haemorrhaging from the national coffers and the threatening sounds coming from Washington and London suggesting the closure of off shore 'tax havens' were annoying and causing concern among investors.

It was with a degree of trepidation that Philip Baverstock went to his meeting at the Treasury. His misgivings were justified.

"Sir Philip I'm afraid I have to organise an examination of your bank's business dealings including an examination of your clients accounts."

"On whose authority?"

"The Lieutenant Governor of these islands as a result of a directive issued by the British Government and the FSA."

"May I remind you that I provided millions of dollars to help with the relief after the hurricane?"

"I'm sure everyone knows that and is grateful, but I don't think that will be sufficient to allow you to avoid this inspection sir."

This situation was a serious setback to his plan which was to empty the bank of all its assets before moving on to the US.

Without the aircraft he would have to use the yacht. That would take time.

92

The Lear Jet touched down at the Owen Roberts airport just as the last rays of daylight faded into the silky darkness of a warm, Cayman evening. Tomorrow the search begins in earnest.

First thing in the morning the party would go to the Police headquarters to start the destruction of one very greedy financier.

Georgetown was full of happy smiling faces, they belonged to holidaymakers, mostly American. The rest of the world was worrying itself silly over the 'Global Financial Crisis'. The balmy weather and unreal surroundings suggested that these islands were avoiding most of the fall out.

Sir Philip Baverstock felt very different when he tried to extract some cash from his own bank. The government official barring his way to the vault cellar was determined that no-one, but absolutely no-one was going to receive any local currency or American dollar from the place until after the financial movement restrictions were removed, and that was not likely to happen in the near future. These restrictions were not directly connected to Baverstock bank or its president but affected them in common with all the other institutions.

International banking was now at a standstill. Philip Baverstock knew that the O'Reillys were on his tail. Time to leave the Island.

With nowhere to hide except on his yacht, he was cursing as he made his way down to the marina and his only mode of escape.

Jonathan had his meeting with the Island's police investigating team.

The locals were loathe to challenge their main benefactor and tried to persuade the British team to 'go easy' on Sir Pip as he was known. After all, his company had paid to build and set up the casino, had invested huge sums in the construction of the airport the marina and numerous smaller businesses which gave the locals well paid jobs. Surely he couldn't possibly have done anything wrong? The investigation which was to come concluded that it was O'Reilly money which had provided the majority of this funding.

The *Cayman Chancer*, at one hundred feet in length was the largest, most luxurious floating extravagance registered in the Island. The crew were delighted to take her out to sea at last.

The motor yacht had been used mainly as a floating conference hotel by its owner the self styled English knight 'Sir Philip Baverstock', ever since he had her delivered two years earlier.

"Where to Sir Pip?" the captain wanted to know.

"Head west Charlie, Florida Keys." He ordered. The yacht surged forward creating a line of white foam in its wake. One hundred and forty three nautical miles later the two powerful marine diesel engines spluttered and died. No orders had been given to fill the fuel tanks or for that matter the fresh water supply, the food freezers or drinks cabinet. The only liquid on board was a plentiful supply of poor quality Kilmona whiskey! The now dry *Cayman Chancer*, was going no further under its own power.

93

Michael and Liam had thoroughly examined the books and records of all the O'Reilly companies and discovered massive discrepancies across every section. The most worrying was the enormous depletion of the pension fund.

This was the one area Sean had been particularly keen to protect over all the years at the airfield. Seeing how it had been plundered by those two slimy creatures almost made him cry, it also made him very, very angry.

The fund was now so depleted that it would not go anywhere near satisfying the retirement needs of the intended recipients. Whatever else happened this would have to be rectified, and urgently. Michael was still trying to discover the whereabouts of the missing managing director of the O'Reilly Group's interests, one William Fraser.

Bill Fraser and his wife Jane, seemed to have evaporated. There was no trace of them in the vicinity of the airport or the village. None of their known friends had seen them or heard from them since the day they vanished. No one near their home had seen any suspicious activity either. Their departure must have taken place in the dead of night. The suspicious nature of this disappearance merited the involvement of the local police. As it was now a week since they vanished,

Michael was able to persuade the station sergeant to initiate a search through all known surveillance cameras. The object of this action was to identify any vehicle leaving the area in the middle of the night. Due to the fact that this was a very quiet area there were few of these cameras operating and a complete blank was drawn as a result.

Bill Fraser had a week's start on his pursuers and he had made good use of this advantage. Jane was told to pack enough clothes for a fortnight's holiday.

They were going to enjoy some sunshine, she wasn't told the destination.

94

The *Cayman Chancer* was dead in the water, not another vessel was in sight. Sir Philip Baverstock was furious!

"Why the hell didn't you fill her up with fuel and water Captain?"

"You didn't give me any notion that we were going on a long trip sir did you? If I had known we were going to Florida I would have needed at least twenty four hours to commission the boat."

"What on earth are we going to do now then?"

"Well sir, first of all I must send out a Mayday signal to alert the authorities to our situation. In the meantime, we should ration our water supplies and warn the crew to stay out of the sun as much as possible. We have no idea how long it will be before we are rescued"

"Absolutely not! There must be no Mayday or any radio signal that will give our position away."

"But sir…"

"No Captain. I insist that we maintain radio silence!"

"You do realise that if I agree with your request I will be breaking maritime law?"

"Bugger *maritime* law! I'm more concerned about *criminal* law. Just do as I say and there will be a bonus for you when we get to Florida."

"You mean *if,* don't you?"

Some quick thinking was needed. If he could contact one of his cronies on Cayman they could organise the delivery of some diesel to be bought to the yacht.

Unfortunately none of his attempts could raise contact He would try again later after he had taken a little nap.

95

The extent of the fraud was now becoming clear. It was also transparent who was mainly responsible. The police put out a warrant for the arrest of Bill Fraser. Now it wasn't only the O'Reillys who were after him. A report of the events leading to the action now being taken in Ireland was sent to the Merseyside Constabulary to initiate the search on the British mainland.

The week's head start would allow anyone time to travel to Australia and back. They could be anywhere. It was soon discovered by checking airline travellers details that Mr and Mrs W. Fraser had booked a one-way first class ticket on British Airways to Vancouver in Canada.

Sir Philip Baverstock had not been put in the frame officially as there was no concrete evidence. The O'Reilly group wanted to make sure of a connection with Fraser before including him. If possible, they would keep it that way. Hopefully by doing their own investigation they would be able to recover some if not all of their cash from this mystery man.

96

On board the yacht things were no longer luxurious. Wallowing in the heavy swell which had developed over the last couple of days made the vessel's movement very uncomfortable, particularly to the one person on board who was not used to spending time at sea. Sir Philip was suffering badly from sea sickness. The Captain became increasingly worried about their predicament. Sure he should have kept the vessel's fuel tank topped up with diesel, but that would have meant the cash he had stolen in lieu of doing this would not have reached the bars in Georgetown via his pocket had he done so. This stupid English gentleman would never have been the wiser. Now they're adrift in the Caribbean heading very slowly for Cuba's beaches, and no power to avoid the rocks on the reef.

Sir Philip's second attempt at contacting someone on Cayman was as fruitless as his first. It was obvious that the word was out that he was now a fugitive.

97

Bill and Jane Fraser enjoyed the luxury of their seats in first class on the big Boeing 747. They had taken advantage of all the goodies on offer ….. Jane didn't realise that this would be the one and only time she would travel like this.

After leaving the airport at Vancouver in the motor-home which Bill had purchased through the magic of the Internet the previous week, they headed for the wilderness. They would certainly be 'away from it all'. as he described the plan to Jane, for the duration of their 'holiday'. Bill knew that once his thieving had been discovered the O'Reillys would pursue him for retribution. Sean wasn't a man to forgive or forget those who treated him badly. The fact that it was Sean's pet 'pension fund' that he had raided so consistently would make him a man with a mission. Those three sons, particularly the muscular Jonathan, would be bound to try to find him, they wouldn't just leave it to the law to deal with. It was imperative he and Jane found a secure hiding place. Somewhere remote but pleasant to spend a year or two. That somewhere was eventually found in the Canadian wilderness. Bill had been planning this escape route for months and had bought a hunter's lodge in the middle of a vast natural forest. It was a lovely spot near a long narrow lake which was bordered by forest. The lake itself was like a dark green mirror as it reflected the foliage of the mass of trees lining its banks on to its perfectly smooth surface. The lodge itself had been fitted to the highest standard available in Canada. There was a refrigerated room attached to the rear of the kitchen which had been filled with every imaginable frozen foodstuff. Logs for the stove had been stacked close to the rear entrance. There were enough provisions for at least a year. After two idyllic weeks motoring around this majestic country they had arrived here. Jane was wondering when they would be retracing their steps.

"Don't you think we ought to start back soon Bill, it's beginning to get so cold outside. What happens if we break down out here?"

"I think you should know that we aren't going back. Well, not yet anyway." he told her.

"What do you mean Bill? not going back, why ever not?"

"I've been a bit naughty old girl. The reason we've been living so well since I took on the job with O'Reilly's business is that I've been borrowing a few bob from the firm's pension fund and they've found out about it. I can't go back without facing a long jail sentence!"

Jane was stunned by this revelation. She couldn't imagine he could do something like that to Sean and Rachel. Two of their best friends. "You *are* joking Bill aren't you?"

"Fraid not luv."

" Just how much have you stolen."

" Two and a half million, give or take a couple of quid"

"*Two and a half million pounds*?"

"Yes. Afraid so!"

"You rotten, lousy bastard!"

"Come off it Jane. You've enjoyed your lifestyle even more than I have."

"I can't believe this. What you've done is despicable. If you had told me about this before we left home I would have told the police!"

267

"And give up your cushy life? I don't think so!"

"I want to go to the nearest police station now. Then you'll see!"

98

Jonathan and his group had now discovered the existence of the *'Cayman Chancer'* and that it had left its berth at the marina and headed out in a westerly direction.

"They're making for the States aren't they?" one of the group remarked.

"Looks like it. We'll have to find out what speed the boat is and try and find her from the air," Jonathan decided.

The Jet was refuelled for a long search. A local fisherman was invited to join them as he knew what the *'Chancer'* looked like. By now the yacht would be very near its destination after its speed had been calculated. The search began after the Lear Jet had reached the Florida shoreline.

It had been agreed that the Keys was the most likely landing place. A yacht like the *Cayman Chancer* would easily lose itself among the dozens of luxury craft moored there. As the jet toured the eastern side of the Florida Keys there were four pairs of binoculars examining every craft afloat. Surely they haven't gone to one of the other Caribbean islands. Maybe they back-tracked after dark and went to Jamaica? stranger still they might have gone to Cuba. Surely not.

It now made sense to have a quick look at the southern shores of Cuba on their search of the waters going back to

Cayman. The pilot of the Lear climbed to fifteen thousand feet so that the crew could scan a larger area on their flight back. They had to stay out of Cuban airspace itself which took them close to where the powerless yacht lay.

"There, there she is!" exclaimed the fisherman member of the searchers.

"Are you certain?" Jonathan enquired. "Oh yes, I'd recognise her anywhere." Now there was another problem for the hunters. Cuba was a no go area for them. Legally anyway. Sean and Rachel were watching events with great interest. They were distressed by the fact that it was possible some of their loyal employees who were also their friends were in danger of losing their jobs, and all because of two very greedy individuals. Sean was now in almost daily contact with his old adversary Derek Jones. Now an old man but a proud one who was as determined as Sean and Rachel to bring his employers to book for the way they had used him by allowing their activities to pass unnoticed. Derek now had full access to Fraser's files. More importantly, he was able to identify the investments Baverstock had and where his contacts worked in the finance industry. These would point the way to recovering substantial funds. There was no stone to be left unturned no corner unexamined and each tiny clue passed on to Sean or Liam for further examination.

On board the *Cayman Chancer* things were getting a little uncomfortable. Sir Pip was still being violently ill. There was little fresh water left in the storage tanks, what there was had to be severely rationed for drinking, which meant there was none to be used for flushing the toilets or washing. The captain was having difficulty in maintaining discipline among a now restless crew. As there was nothing they could do to move the vessel they set two sea anchors to arrest their progress towards the inner reef. The captain's hope was that these anchors would be able to hold until Sir Philip realised that they needed assistance from an outside source, probably Cuban!

The crew was becoming aggressive. They all knew what needed to be done, but the stupid Englishman didn't seem to. The steward decided that the crew should be offered a spot of calming fluid.

He broke out a crate of Kilmona Whiskey which was well received, so was the next crate and the next........ It didn't take them long to become completely incapable of causing trouble! As soon as Philip Baverstock fell asleep after his latest bout of sea sickness the Captain sent out his Mayday signal. Essential help would soon be on its way whether Sir Philip flaming Baverstock wanted it or not! The Mayday signal was picked up by a U.S. Coastguard fast craft which was patrolling the outer limits of its sweep. Maybe this was another drugs run gone wrong. With luck.

Jonathan was listening to the emergency frequency on the aircraft's radio and heard the Mayday from the *Cayman Chancer.*

"So. The engine's conked out. Can you get in touch with the coastguard from the aircraft?" Jonathan asked.

"I think so. Let me check the maritime frequencies."

"If you can contact them, give them the information we've got will you.

Maybe they can arrest the yacht, or at least suggest they take the boat into a friendly port where we can have Baverstock apprehended."

The pilot spent a few minutes scanning the likely frequencies before announcing that he had picked up a transmission from a coastguard vessel communicating with its base in the Florida Keys.

The officer reported that they had intercepted the Mayday from the rogue yacht requesting assistance. The reply from the shore station ordered them to board the yacht and tow it back to the Cayman Islands where they could examine it properly. If it was an innocent vessel its owners could effect repairs and resume its cruising. Jonathan told the pilot of the Lear Jet to keep listening in, but say nothing to the Coastguards, yet.

"Roger. Copy that." Ended the transmission.

The fast craft pulled alongside the anchored yacht and secured a tow-line.

After passing some fresh drinking water to the captain to distribute to his crew before starting the long tow back to Grand Cayman where, unknown to the Customs officers, the police would love to see them.

Sir Philip Baverstock started to protest to the American Customs officers until the yacht's captain put his finger to his lips in a silencing gesture. Sir Pip took the hint and buttoned his own!

99

Bill Fraser was trying to persuade Jane to accept the situation and support him in what he wanted to do next. She pretended to get over the shock of what he had told her, his threatening behaviour had frightened her. Here in this wilderness there was no-one she could approach for help. If she could make him believe she had relented and now would try to get to enjoy the awesome scenery which surrounded them he might make a mistake and give her the chance to escape the dreadful loneliness and fear he had inflicted on her.

This was the person everyone loved. He was trusted totally by their friends. How could he behave like this? She had been in love with him ever since that first meeting at the college dance all those years ago. Now she was afraid of him. It was as though he'd had a brainstorm, and she was being forced to share this nightmare. Somehow she knew she would have to find a way of contacting Sean or John Shepherd to tell them where she was and what her husband was trying to do, but how? In the meantime she was going to have to become an actress and a very convincing one at that!

"We can't stay here forever Bill can we ?"

"Nope. I have had an idea I think you'll like!" Bill Fraser had been giving their situation much thought over the last few days.

The motor home would have to be disposed of. The only vehicle dealer he could find was three hours drive away near a logging village. When they arrived at this place the dealer enjoyed making a deal involving the exchange of a practically new Winnebago camper for a well used second (or third) hand four by four Chevrolet utility vehicle.

"I don't get much call for these things up here" was the answer to Bill's suggestion that some cash aught to balance things up a bit. As they drove away from Honest Joe's dealership they could observe through the trees a large campsite with row upon row of logger's homes.. mostly similar Winnebagos!

They had now been away from his crime scene for over three weeks. Time which would have been put to good use by his pursuers no doubt.

He could almost see his one-time friend searching his abandoned home in Ireland looking for clues to his present whereabouts. Naturally Jane would be included in the negative thoughts in the O'Reilly collective minds. A pity that.

Rachel is a gorgeous spirited woman for whom he had a certain respect. Her boring husband though was such an easy mark. To trust anyone so totally without doing any preliminary checking up was quite beyond comprehension or respect. If he hadn't made it so easy to divert those millions. If he had made it a bit of a challenge things might have been different. It wasn't a bad existence really. His was a generous salary. He didn't *need* to steal. Too late to concern himself now, what was done could not easily be undone. The game now was to stay ahead of the enemy! Canada was a wonderfully complete country in which to play hide and go seek.

Jane was feeling very miserable now. She had been in love with this man for over forty years. Suddenly she loathed the sight of him. How could he think she would want to live this sort of existence?

"It won't be forever Jane. As soon as things quieten down over there we'll go back."

They both knew that this would never happen. Jane also knew that she would have to leave Bill as soon as possible and return to 'face the music', which would probably be very loud and probably tuneless.

A week after arriving in this desolate place which had no shops, no cinema or village. Not even a single neighbour to call on. It did have a lake full of fish, apparently waiting for Bill to catch! The only 'visitor' was the little float plane which settled on the lake occasionally. Hardly paradise for a wealthy couple. .

I⊘⊘

Derek Jones had been putting in fourteen hour days since Fraser's disappearance, his efforts were producing some promising leads. Having searched through the bank's employment records he had established a chain of high profile appointments for Sir Philip Baverstock, Mr Hugh Watson and Mr John Shepherd all at directorship level in private banks and industry.

The identity of these individuals who were now known to be the same man, corresponded to other aliases. A certain Mr Baver was CEO of a German merchant bank and a Roger Stock was financial director of a company in Belgium specialising in 'Hedge' funds. It didn't take Derek Jones long to discover that Baver and Stock were one and the same! This guy was some operator.

Derek's persistence paid handsomely when he discovered this slippery individual's real identity. By chance whilst trawling through his paperwork he came across an application to open a bank account in the Isle of Man where the office insisted on verifiable proof of identity by way of a passport facsimile.

This showed a photograph of 'Sir' Philip Baverstock alias John Shepherd alias Hugh Watson and goodness knows how many other aliases he had used, turned out to be one Victor

Harvey. There didn't seem to be any record anywhere of Victor Harvey's activities. No criminal record existed either. Not so much as a speeding ticket. The character when 'off duty' from criminal capers was squeaky clean!

It was a much easier tracing job with bank accounts in this name and there was an incredible number of accounts in so many banks and businesses where the name Victor Harvey had accumulated an enormous fortune. Every transaction depositing cash into banks or buying bonds came from respectable sources. When Michael was given this information he started calculating the debt owed to the O'Reilly group of companies. There had to be a way of confiscating this and returning it to the pension fund where it belonged. First the culprit had to be detained. At least they now knew where he was.

Bill Fraser was another matter and probably a more difficult target as so far they hadn't a clue where he was.

This was about to change!

I Ø I

Jane Fraser was acting the part of the loyal wife very effectively, pandering to each of her husband's demands. Cooking his disgusting fish when he caught the odd one. They had no idea what breed of creature they were eating. Mostly they had a revolting taste and the texture left a good deal to be desired, however Bill pretended to enjoy these meals. Jane also pretended to find them palatable. It was only going to be a matter of time before her chance to escape would present itself.

Moving into the lodge was at least a vast improvement on the restrictions imposed by the mobile home. The worst part of her predicament was knowing that they were both considered pariahs to their friends Sean and Rachel. Her misery was compounded by the remoteness of her surroundings. It was always bitterly cold. Most days it either snowed or rained heavily. The grey overcast sky matched her constant feeling of depression.

Having traded in the motor home for the four by four utility vehicle, their presence to any passing traveller or store owner would not invite curiosity.

The long round trip to the nearest settlement - Bear Creek for supplies always passed without comment. Jane knew her only chance to get a message to the outside world was going to have to be via this isolated settlement, but how to do it ? Bill never let her out of his sight! After the way she had reacted when he confessed to his stealing Bill knew he couldn't trust her to remain loyal to him. Much as he still loved her, his love for money was greater and would determine his behaviour towards her. He would have to keep a close watch on her actions now. Still, for the moment he didn't have to worry as they were miles from any human habitation. Bill had had no contact from outside. Victor hadn't been in touch on the phone which surprised him. He was sure any urgent action by the O'Reilly team would be relayed to him in this way. His mobile phone was the very latest satellite variety and was active anywhere in the world. Silence as far as Bill was concerned, was security.

1ø2

The *Cayman Chancer* was nearing its home port under tow from the U.S. Customs cutter. The *Chancer's* captain was a crafty operator, he realised that if the yacht was towed into the inner reaches of the harbour there would be little chance of his boss dodging the inevitable contact with the police.

"Our mooring will have been taken by now," he told the customs man who was sharing the bridge with him.

"I think we'd better anchor in the bay so that the refuelling boat can come alongside."

The young customs officer radioed his own vessel to explain this to his senior.

"Roger, copy that." came the standard reply. As soon as this acknowledgement was received orders were given to summon the refuelling vessel to proceed to the rendezvous anchorage out in the bay. When this action was complete and both vessels anchored, the captain made his excuse to 'relieve' himself and left the bridge. As soon as he was out of sight and sound of the customs officials he hurried down to 'Sir' Pip's stateroom.

"Quick, put on the uniform which is in the wardrobe sir. When the oiler comes alongside we'll get you on board as a

Sharing the Trough

ship's officer. Here's my cap, pull it well down over your face when I give you the nod."

Victor wasn't slow to catch on to the idea which allowed him the chance to get a step ahead of the pursuers. If he could contact Bill Fraser, who has disappeared, he may be able to help him do likewise. The uniform wasn't a perfect fit, but then if it was he would have stood out as a very unlikely private yachtsman. Most of these were somewhat corpulent in stature and generally grubby and scruffy in appearance. Victor observed his reflection in the full length mirror and was satisfied that the food stains on the whitish trousers and the wine dribbles on the jacket were genuine and should allow his escape without too much scrutiny. When the refuelling vessel came alongside the crew secured the lines and commenced the refuelling process.

Whilst this was taking place, Victor Harvey 'jumped ship' and hid himself among the pipes, pumps and assorted gear associated with the boat's operation.

After half an hour the yacht was ready to make its own way into Grand Cayman harbour.

As soon as they were under weigh the customs officer on board the yacht asked where Mr Baverstock was . The yacht's skipper explained that his boss had been suffering badly with sea sickness and was resting in his suite. When the Customs officer went to check on him he heard loud groaning coming from inside the suite whose door was locked. The engineer pretending to be the sick passenger was making a fair impression of a very unhealthy body!

103

"Hello, yes? Oh hello Victor. How are things going over there. Have the O'Reillys made any progress with their probing?" Bill Fraser enquired after answering his Satellite phone's ring.

"Fraid so. They have already seized the two aircraft and have managed to get the funds in Baverstock bank frozen. I can't transfer that last bundle of cash. There is a general hunt for me here in Cayman. So far I've been able to keep a step ahead but I'm going to have to get off the Island very soon. I know most of the gang at the airport. I'm confident I'll be able to get away so long as it's within the next couple of days."

"Where are you going to head for? You can't go back to U.K. or Ireland, they'll be sure to be watching out for you. How about Brazil or Mexico?"

"No good. I won't be able to get at the funds south of the border. It will have to be the U.S. or Canada. I can probably transfer most of the cash into my own name if I can 'get lost' in either country."

"Well, Jane and I have this place near Bear Creek which is miles from civilisation. Why don't you stay with us until you get sorted out? If you get a flight to Vancouver I can drive down to meet you"

"That sounds good Bill. I'll get myself organised and fly over sometime later this week. As soon as I can get a flight I'll give you another call. OK?

"Fine Victor. If I were you I'd come Air Canada rather than BA. Be sure also to get a standard ticket rather your usual first class. that way you'll draw less attention to yourself."

"Good thinking. Be in touch. Cheers."

1Ø4

Paddy was enjoying the revival of the Kilmona distillery. The ever increasing sales had earned him the sort of fortune Bill Fraser and Victor Harvey couldn't even dream of. He couldn't care less about the money really, he had never been a slave to it. Now that he was extremely wealthy he thought it was time to put some of it back into the community following the example set by his friend and mentor Sean O'Reilly. The Kilmona Deprived Children Holiday Fund was set up which was Paddy's way of making sure that any Irish child from a broken home or deprived family would have the opportunity to experience visits to countries and cultures children from their background would not normally enjoy. This organisation enjoyed enormous success.

Rachel and Sean were supportive and delighted for Paddy.

What a long way they had all come from the gate of Crumlin Road jail all those years ago!

A strong bond had developed between them during this time. Paddy had avoided the 'marriage trap' and had been hitched to his sweetheart... Kilmona Potcheen with few disagreements since the introduction to Nellie after his cell-mate's phone call to him following his release.

He counted his blessings every morning as he awoke and again before he went to bed each night. The evening version was usually a little blurred.

I Ø 5

The call came from Victor asking Bill to meet him from the airport the following day.

Sean had given instructions to his team to allow the two crooks to meet and only intercept them after they had left the airport building. He wanted to be the one to surprise the pair of them. It was important to deal with these two separately. Bill was definitely going to be arrested and charged. The slimy Victor Harvey was a different matter. The way he had tried to con Nellie, bullied Derek Jones, stolen the future for all those employees and tried to swindle Paddy and himself deserved a wholly different future. Sean and Rachel had devised a programme of punishment to fit his crimes. Prison was not their choice for him. Sean and Rachel had other plans! Although gaol was always going to be an alternative if their plans didn't work out.

The team was apprehensive. Canada is a big country. If the two fugitives gave them the slip now it might take months if not years to track them down. Bill Fraser was a slick operator. Having been able to swindle them so successfully for so long he would be a formidable opponent and was undoubtedly going to resist attempts to be captured.

They were going to have to proceed with the utmost caution if they were going to be successful.

1Ø6

Victor Harvey dressed as a scruffy yachtsman slipped easily from the luxurious *Cayman Chancer* luxury vessel to the dirty marine oiler and the rest of his life. Even here on Cayman Island where he had been regarded as something of a hero for the past ten years he was having to hide. Word was out that he was being pursued by a powerful team. It was not known yet however, what the crimes he was accused of were. He still had one or two contacts of dubious trustworthiness that he could rely on.

During his visits to these Islands he had bribed generously, the most influential officials who ran things including the airport director. He was going to have to bribe this individual one last time…..It was getting very urgent that he remove himself to a much bigger country in which to get himself lost. With Bill Fraser's help Canada would be his destination. This final, very expensive bribe resulted in his possession of an airline ticket one way to Vancouver via Air Canada in the name of Joseph Bloggs which was an unusually obvious pseudonym for an expert in deception like Victor. He reckoned that this would help to put officials off his track.

Included with the ticket was a U.S. passport. All this achieved in twenty four hours. "I'll be on the two thirty five

Air Canada flight out of Grand Cayman for 'you know where' tomorrow Bill. Will you meet me there?"

"I'll do my best Victor, it will depend on the weather. If there's no more snow overnight it should be OK However at this time of year it will probably take me the best part of a week to get there should a snow storm develop. You can always stay in one of the airport hotels until I get there."

"Thanks Bill, I'll see you soon. Bye."

I Ø 7

Derek Jones was excited with the news he received from his contact at the telephone company. During his search of Fraser's office he came across the contract his target had made for the use of a satellite mobile phone. A quick call to the Fraud Squad detectives soon had this this monitored and recorded.

When Sean was informed of this development he asked the officers to take no action until they could get a 'fix' on the location of this instrument which could only happen when it was transmitting. When the call was made by Victor Harvey the 'target' was pin-pointed to a spot in the wilderness of Canada. Bill and Victor had made their first mistake. All the waiting hunters had to do was wait a little longer... Until the next call from Victor.

The satellite call was duly intercepted and the contents passed from his contact to Derek Jones who immediately forwarded the details on to Sean who was awaiting any information in his hotel room in Vancouver. The call came from Derek Jones telling him that Victor had asked Bill to meet him at the airport the following day. Sean's team should be in place at Vancouver airport in plenty of time. The waiting was a little frustrating but at last the end of the search was near.

The hotel was a very comfortable place with the amenities which were available to its guests. A swimming pool, sauna and gymnasium all taken advantage of by Sean. He was in almost constant touch with Rachel and his sons who were now all on their way to visit Canada!

"Hello darling we're all set. Liam and the twins are already on their way to the airport where I shall join them. Derek is keeping a close watch this end.

Any new information he gets he says he'll pass on directly to you." Rachel stated.

"Good. I'm looking forward so much to this re-union. Once we have the buggers on the ropes we'll start recovery procedures but we'd better not count chickens yet. Those two will be pretty desperate I'm sure and dangerous with it."

"Please be careful Sean darling. Now that we've stopped the rot we can start to re-build the funds with our existing businesses can't we?"

"Yes of course, don't you worry your lovely self about me. I'm a big boy now!"

They both chuckled but Rachel's concern sounded in her voice.

"See you shortly love".

I∅8

Victor disguised himself as best he could by dressing with typical holiday-makers loud shirt, wide brimmed Tilley hat pulled down low over his eyes and thick rimmed dark glasses. This wouldn't stand close scrutiny but was sufficient to allow him access to the flight to Canada. He took his seat at the rear of the Boeing triple seven aircraft. The window seat he occupied wasn't what he was used to. It was too small and damned uncomfortable.

How could the 'plebs' put up with this kind of torture every time they went off on their nasty little holidays? It was incomprehensible. Six and a half hours worth of sheer purgatory was promised after the aircraft took off.

The uncertain conclusion of this trip was unsettling. Victor Harvey was used to being in control. He would make it his business to re-instate himself as master of his destiny as soon as he got off this infernal crowd shifter! The plastic food thrown at him did nothing to improve his comfort. Neither did the sniffing and snorting of the fat gossipy grandmother sitting in the seat next to him. Oh God. This is going to be a hellish trip. They had only been airborne a couple of hours.

Bill Fraser was keen to get to the airport and whisk the risky 'visitor' away from suspicious eyes as soon as practicable. He didn't like having to do this at all. The only trouble was he wouldn't be able to 'persuade' his old boss to transfer any more funds unless he could control his movements. An interesting confrontation was imminent.

The Air Canada flight was nearly an hour late arriving in Vancouver. The hundred knot head wind had done its best to make Victor's discomfort as painful as possible. It was a very irritable fugitive who caught Sean's searching gaze as he entered the arrivals hall clutching the handle of his wheeled Delsey case.

Sean spoke into his mobile phone as he recognised his target.

"He's arrived boys. He looks a little tired. An easy target to follow, he's wearing a very colourful shirt with a pattern of palm tree foliage across the front and the legend 'I'm the greatest babe magnet' in yellow letters on his back. He's moving towards the exit now. Have you got him Liam?"

"Yes dad, I'll follow him until mum spots him then I'll make my way to the pick-up point."

"Where's Michael? is he in the car?"

"Yes. He's ready to follow Fraser as soon as we eyeball him."

"Has Jonathon started his move to Bear Creek do you know?"

"I think so. He should be about half way there by now."

"Good. Great!"

I Ø 9

Jane Fraser was playing the supportive wife to Bill as they drove the utility Chevrolet towards Vancouver airport. It was difficult keeping up the pretence of affection for this thief now driving the vehicle at high speed.

The needle on the speedometer was nudging eighty miles per hour. Conditions on the road were suitable for half that speed by a formula one driver!

The snow was packed hard in between the wheel tracks where the heavy timber vehicles had compressed the stuff into icy tramlines. The road was very straight allowing the vehicle to remain upright and more or less following its general direction.

The trip was frightening and uncomfortable to the unfortunate female passenger. Jane knew she had to refrain from showing her concern for their safety. Bill's determination to reach their destination in the shortest possible time was testing the vehicle, his driving and her nerves to the limit.

When finally, they came to a halt, there was an audible sigh coming from the frantic engine as its cooling process began. Bill told Jane to stay in the car until their 'guest' was safely on board and they could retrace their route to Bear Creek.

Liam watched Victor as he left the Terminal and walked towards him at the pick-up point. The phone he was carrying was ready to ring Michael as soon as Fraser arrived. Victor Harvey was shivering with the sub zero temperature when Bill arrived twenty minutes after he had left the warmth of the arrivals hall.

He wasted no time in getting into the car and Bill wasted even less in slipping the gear lever into 'drive'. They were on their way.

Rachel had kept her gaze on Victor and had followed him out of the building.

She quickly opened Michael's passenger door as soon as the vehicle came to a stop. The final pursuit had begun with Jonathon well ahead to pick up the trail as soon as the Chevrolet approached the outskirts of Bear Creek. Michael soon picked up the tail lights of his target which was cruising at a far more comfortable forty miles per hour. There was no need to rush now.

"Are you sure you weren't followed Victor? There wasn't an O'Reilly on the plane was there?"

"I can't say for certain as I couldn't observe the first or business class people but I don't think so." Victor responded without conviction.

"I doubt there was. I can't see that bunch spending on comfort can you?" Bill stated.

The conversation ended with first Victor and then Jane falling asleep. They were both exhausted. Bill was relying on adrenaline to keep him awake for the next four hours.

The following O'Reilly justice squad were still fresh and ready for whatever was ahead. As the two vehicles left the suburbs of Vancouver and headed north towards the end of the trail, the highway lost most of its traffic. Michael was watching the tail lights of his quarry proceeding ahead of him. There was no need to follow too closely and so he allowed the maximum visual distance to exist between them. Half an hour after Michael had picked up his mother outside the airport he noticed the lights of another vehicle in his rear view mirror. If he allowed this machine to overtake him it would appear natural to the driver of the car ahead if he had noticed he was being followed. Slowly the other car drew up behind him. Rachel's mobile phone rang soon after this. "Hi darling, it's only your beloved and your eldest son in the car behind you"

"Michael suggests you overtake us so that it will put Bill off the scent if he has noticed us following him."

"Good thinking Mike. Speed up a little to get closer. Make sure he sees us doing it."

The convoy continued into the night. Snow had started falling now. The three vehicles gradually got closer together as the lead car of Bill's slowed for the poor visibility. The journey back to Bear Creek took almost seven hours. The late dawn was beginning to usher in the last hours of the chase. The fresh fall of snow left the countryside pristine in its virginal blanket. The road itself had narrowed to single carriageways as they approached the tiny hamlet.

Jonathan's car was sitting outside the general store with its dusting of snow hiding the driver patiently waiting inside.

As Michael's car passed him Jonathan started his own vehicle and moved off to join the others, all of the following vehicles staying out of sight of the target. Its wheel-tracks were leaving a clear trail to follow.

II∅

The tyre tracks turned off the road after what seemed an age in time. In reality it was thirty five minutes. Sean stopped his car short of this turning waited for Michel to pull up behind him then the O'Reilly family left their warm cars to proceed on foot towards the log cabin just visible through the trees.

"See if you can get round the back of the place Jonny, in case either of them decides to do a runner." Sean instructed. "Gotcher" Jonathan replied moving off into the cover of the snow laden fir trees.

"Mike, Stay here with Mum. Give me five minutes, or any loud sound from the house. Then come and join the party!"

"OK Dad." Sean made his way to the cabin, dodging from tree to tree. Stopping every few steps to see if he could observe any movement from the building. All was quiet. It seemed that they hadn't been observed. The utility vehicle was sitting in front of the doorway offering Sean cover for the final sprint to the entrance. He was about to grasp the handle to open the door when it was jerked open......

Bill was standing just inside. He grabbed Sean's jacket and hauled him inside with one movement kicking the door shut afterwards. Sean hadn't forgotten what a big strong individual Bill was. "Hello old friend, welcome to Wilderness farm!" he snarled at Sean. "A little less of the 'old friend' you disgusting creep. You know why I'm here don't you?"

"I imagine you're under the illusion that I'm going to fall over and go back to Ireland with you. Yes?"

"Oh no Bill. I don't expect any kind of co-operation from you after the systematic thieving you've been doing over all these years. I just want you to tell me why you felt you had to do it?"

"You made me do it you idiot. With your unquestioning trust in someone you knew nothing about! To begin with, it was just a question of taking over control which was so easy. After that the money came pouring in thanks to *my* efforts. Why should you pig farmers get all that credit for what I achieved?"

But why steal from the pension fund ? What did all those fine people who did the *real* work do to offend you so much?"

"They didn't offend me, they were so gullible that they deserved no better!" Jane came into the room from the kitchen having heard nothing of this exchange. Saw Sean standing in front of her and her face showed the shame she felt as his gaze settled on her.

"Hello Sean." She mumbled. "It's good to see you." Bill stared at her and shouted; "Shut up you silly bitch. Do you think he's here for a garden party?"

Sean stared at this man he'd been so fond of for so long and wondered how someone with the talent he obviously had could have got life so totally wrong.

Bill casually reached up and removed his hunting rifle from its cradle above the fireplace.

"No, Mr Pigsmith. I am certainly not going to come back to Ireland or anywhere else with you."

Bill Fraser put the rifle to his shoulder and aimed it at Sean's head........

III

The sound of the rifle shot brought the rest of the O'Reilly family rushing into the dwelling as fast as they could move. The back door opened a split second before Michael, Liam and Rachel crashed in through the main entrance.

On the floor with blood pouring from a head wound lay the still figure of Bill Fraser...Before he had been able to pull the trigger of the gun, Jane had smashed him over the head with a bottle of Bill's favourite Champagne, smashing it and knocking him spark out! The fizzy, sparkling contents of the green bottle cascaded over its main recipient as he fell. The rifle fell from his hands and discharged itself as its butt struck the floor. The bullet intended for Sean ricocheted from the steel chain supporting the ceiling light fitting and struck the wall bracket holding a stuffed moose's head. This had been a magnificent specimen of the local wildlife before being converted into a hunter's trophy.

The antlers protruding from the creature's head measured a good two metres from tip to tip. The dislodgement by the lead missile of its supporting hook caused the trophy to fall forwards.... When it came to rest on the floor it straddled the prostrate figure of Bill Fraser effectively trapping him in the cage of these antlers.

"Did you know he had been stealing from us Jane?"

"Only after we came here Rachel. I would have left him and told you both straight away if I had known before. I hate him and what he's done to us all. I think he would have killed me if you hadn't come.

What are you going to do with him now?"

Jane was sobbing quietly now. Relief that her nightmare was finally over, but most of the tears were those of relief that Rachel and Sean now knew she had had no part in the deception and fraud.

"He is going to jail for a long time Jane, the severity of his crimes will make sure of that.

The silent figure of Victor Harvey stared first at the trapped unconscious figure on the floor, then he gazed at the gathered O'Reilly family now blocking both the doorways. Any possibility of escape remote. Like all bullies, Victor was an accomplished coward. His attempt to distance his own behaviour from his accomplice Bill, fell on collective deaf ears.

II2

Victor Harvey clearly heard what was said and he knew that his fate would be similar if his lawyers were unable to distance him from his partner's corruption. When Bill Fraser regained conciousness, Jane had bathed his head wound and bandaged him leaving him trapped under the moose head. It was a convenient 'holding pen' rendering him powerless should he be inclined to attempt any further harm to his ex colleagues.

It would take the police some time to get to this remote spot. Time enough to sort out Mr Victor Harvey's new contract....

"I have no doubt your slimy lawyers will do their utmost to wring a lenient sentence for you Hugh, or is it Sir Philip? No?

Maybe it's John. I tell you what. We'll have this contract made out in your real name shall we? Victor Harvey... If you agree to *all* my demands you *may* be allowed to keep some of your *legally* gained cash at the end of your contract. If you don't, we'll use all the evidence that Derek Jones has gathered against you.

You must be aware that if this is the route we take you will go to prison for much longer than this swine." Sean said gesticulating towards the scowling figure lying on the floor.

"You don't give me much choice. Alright you win I agree, although I think you are being unreasonable!"

Victor's whingeing voice was loaded with regret at being caught. The humiliation caused by that little twerp at the bank. - Jones, was almost too much.

Sean and Rachel had prepared the contract for Victor Harvey very carefully with a lot of help from Derek Jones. The following afternoon was spent on Bill Fraser's computer transferring all Victor Harvey's illicit fortune into the Pension fund from which most of it was stolen. There was surprisingly little left after this action. Not enough to live comfortably and there would certainly not be room for any luxuries.

The final and most important part of the contract was left until last as a surprise for Victor Harvey, he was to be employed full time by the O'Reilly group of companies back home in Ireland!

Because of the complexity of his financial skill, he was going to be a useful asset to the O'Reilly group, always providing he was constantly monitored.

The contract was to last without possibility of breaking by Harvey, for five years. His humiliation should be complete at its completion.

Any attempt to renege on the conditions laid down in the contract would activate criminal proceedings with an inevitable jail sentence.

113

When the family group had returned to Ireland after the settling of accounts, Rachel and Sean were relaxing in their lovely home.

"You know what I'd like to do darling wife," Sean said as he handed her a glass of cheap supermarket wine.

"No dear, I've no idea what you'd like to do. Do tell me?"

" I'd like to get some Gloucester Old Spot and some Wessex saddlebacks and start the old job again. Just as a hobby" Rachel looked over to him under those delicious eyelashes which were now grey, and replied;

"What a great idea! could we do that Sean, could we really do that?" The excitement lit up her still beautiful face.

"Why not? The boys have taken complete control of the companies and the pig pens will be OK with a little bit of attention.

If we sell all the female progeny for breeding, just fatten the boars for meat it should be fun and will keep us out of mischief when we're not looking after the Council constituents."

"Just a small problem with the idea darling."

Rachel had frown lines on her face.

"Which is?" Sean queried.

"We'll have to employ some help". Rachel responded. "I've thought about that love. It's all in hand".

114

Bill Fraser was charged with theft on a gigantic scale. He was found guilty at his trial and was committed to serve fifteen years in jail. His assets were confiscated and the proceeds of the sale were distributed to his creditors including the Pension fund which was now able to look after all the employees generously.

Parole would not be considered until he had served at least twelve years of his sentence, which meant he would probably die in there. Jane received a good settlement out of the legitimate savings of her husband. She gratefully rekindled her friendship with the O'Reillys and helped them with their charity work.

I I 5

Rachel and Sean had the time of their lives following the chase after the fugitives. Restarting the breeding unit with the introduction of rare breeds of pig had them travelling the length and breadth of the British Isles obtaining the best examples of each type of animal. Gloucester Old Spots, Tamworths, Essex and Wessex Saddlebacks were all selected from the best breeders regardless of cost. By the time this buying spree was completed they had the most comprehensive collection in the British Isles. This would be a valuable conservation unit. One in which they could take immense pride. They were aware that there was likely to be little or no profit to be made. This would not be a business to them as it was to be their hobby.

"When you've finished cleaning out the porkers you can start at the top farrowing house. After that if there's time, you can fill all the feed trolleys.

Tomorrow we have to weigh those porkers and move three pregnant sows from the top paddock into the pens you scrubbed out yesterday."

Sean was issuing the daily orders to the new stockman for jobs needing to be done on the farm. There was always so much to do and the days were always full.

Rachel and Sean visited the farrowing houses every evening to watch the babies in the light of their infra red heaters. This was still the most wonderful way to spend time particularly as they were no longer required to do the physical work themselves.

Sheila Ferguson was a regular visitor who loved these creatures almost as much as the O'Reillys.

"I'll do the feeding this weekend." She volunteered. This would allow her the chance to get really close to them. It had been such a long time since the last time she had been involved. Sheila was now, like her original employers retired and revelling in the chance to 'play' with these gorgeous creatures. She needed no prompting to lend a hand in this way occasionally.

Sean reluctantly agreed to her proposal as the regular keeper was still learning the basics of stock keeping and needed all the experience he could get doing the chores.

Rachel noticed the new helper slowly strolling towards where they stood. He didn't seem to be the most enthusiastic stockman.

"A volunteer is going to do the weekend feeding so you can have this weekend off." She told him.

The figure's step quickened noticeably when he heard this very welcome news.

"Please be sure to be on time on Monday, the animals know what time they should be getting breakfast!" The reluctant farmhand scowled at the remark. 'Bloody pigs! I hate the filthy things. I hate these peasant farmers.' were some of the mumbled thoughts emanating from the miserable looking labourer as he walked away. Sean was in earshot for most of this diatribe.

"I can't understand this attitude of yours Victor, after all you've been sharing the trough with them for years!" He said.

Victor Harvey had only just begun his 'sentence' and was already bitterly regretting having targeted the O'Reilly enterprises to expand his now extinct fortune! Five years from now he should be a reformed character. Rachel and Sean were determined to make this time a lesson in humility for Victor whilst using his financial genius to produce funds for the benefit of the local community.

"You're not going to believe this Sean." They heard the familiar voice from the unexpected visitor as he stepped out of his Land Rover.

"Go on Paddy. We're listening." Sean answered

" I've found a new use for the 'special' potcheen!"

" Really?"

"I accidentally spilled some of the stuff on the concrete outside the distillery. It dissolved it!…. Left a neat hole right through to the soil underneath. I reckon we could make a fortune flogging it to the building trade!"

Sean and Rachel couldn't control their amusement on hearing this.

"You go right ahead pal. Some of that would have come in handy in Crumlin Road!" Victor Harvey's ears pricked up as he heard this revelation.

He still had no idea of the secret formula and so his frustration was going to escalate.

When they were alone again after the departure of Paddy and Victor, Sean had a wistful look on his face.

"Rachel," he said at the end of another satisfying day; "how about taking that 'rain check' today."

"What rain check was that Sean.?"

"The one you promised me the day I proposed to you!" They laughed again together, kissed and strolled over to see what the boars were doing!